Jim Thorpe

Olympic Champion

Illustrated by Gray Morrow

Jim
Thorpe

Olympic Champion

by Guernsey Van Riper, Jr.

Aladdin Paperbacks

Aladdin Paperbacks
An imprint of Simon & Schuster Children's Publishing Division
1230 Avenue of the Americas, New York, NY 10020
First Aladdin Paperbacks edition, 1986
Printed in the United States of America

10   9   8   7
Library of Congress Cataloging-in-Publication Data

Van Riper, Guernsey, 1909–
   Jim Thorpe, Olympic champion.

   Reprint. Originally published: Indianapolis :
Bobbs-Merrill, c1983.
   Summary: A biography of the American Indian known as
one of the best all-round athletes in history, for his
accomplishments as an Olympic medal winner as well as an
outstanding professional football and baseball player.
   1. Thorpe, Jim, 1887–1953—Juvenile literature.
2. Athletes—United States—Biography—Juvenile
literature.   [1. Thorpe, Jim, 1887–1953.   2. Athletes.
3. Indians of North America—Biography]   I. Morrow,
Gray, ill.   II. Title.
[GV697.T5V36   1986]   796'.092'4 [B] [92]   86-10792
ISBN 0-02-042140-0 (pbk.)

For
D. Laurance Chambers
in gratitude and affection

Illustrations

Numerous smaller illustrations

Contents

CHILDHOOD OF FAMOUS AMERICANS

★   ★

Books by Guernsey Van Riper, Jr.

BABE RUTH: ONE OF BASEBALL'S GREATEST
JIM THORPE: OLYMPIC CHAMPION
KNUTE ROCKNE: YOUNG ATHLETE
LOU GEHRIG: ONE OF BASEBALL'S GREATEST
RICHARD BYRD: BOY WHO BRAVED THE UNKNOWN
WILL ROGERS: YOUNG COWBOY

★ ★ ★ Jim
Thorpe

Olympic Champion

Bright Path

SLOWLY Jimmy Thorpe raised an arrow and fitted it to his bow.

Twenty feet away, in the fork of a hickory tree, a red squirrel was gnawing on a nut.

The little Indian boy took careful aim. He pulled back the bowstring, ever so slowly, and then released the arrow.

Whisht—thud! The arrow hit the tree just below the squirrel's perch.

Jimmy caught only a glimpse of the bushy tail disappearing on the other side of the tree. Then higher up the trunk the squirrel appeared. It chattered at the boy, scolding, then darted away through the treetops. High in a nearby tree the saucy squirrel appeared again. It seemed to dare Jimmy to try again. Then it was gone.

Jimmy frowned. "Something is wrong. That arrow didn't go where I aimed it," he thought. "I'll never get to go on a long deer hunt with Pa if I can't shoot better."

The five-year-old boy picked up his arrow. He stood listening, looking all around him. His quick eyes saw the bushes tremble over to his left. There was a rustling, as something moved through dry leaves. Out into the open waddled a fat possum. To Jimmy's surprise the animal headed straight toward him.

Jimmy was very excited. He raised his bow.

But the possum stopped. It just stood there, its little red eyes glaring up at Jimmy.

With a puzzled frown, Jimmy lowered his bow. *"Hey-yo, Ai-yani,"* he said. "Say, Mr. Possum, how can I shoot you if you just walk up to meet me? That isn't the way to hunt. I'm supposed to sneak up on you!"

He waved his bow. "Go on, run!" he called.

The possum showed its teeth, like a dog snarling, but it didn't make a sound.

"All right, all right, *Ai-yani*, I won't come any closer. I don't want you to bite me!"

The Indian boy stood quietly. After a moment the possum turned and started away. It waddled along without looking to one side or the other. The coarse hair stood out all over its body. Its bare tail trailed along behind, like a huge rat's tail. The possum shuffled through the dry leaves and grass with a great rustling noise.

"Why, I'd think all the possums would be killed by now. I never saw anything so dumb! I won't shoot anything so easy, though."

He glanced around again. Jimmy's eyes always looked half closed, but they didn't miss a single movement about him. His sharp ears caught every small sound in the woods. Only songbirds were moving in the trees. Only the breeze stirred, blowing gently in his face.

Then something moved far ahead. Jimmy's quick eyes spotted it instantly. Something was hiding in a thick clump of bushes. Jimmy caught a glimpse of a bronzed body. Then it disappeared. Jimmy grinned. "It's Charlie! I'll surprise him."

He picked a haw apple from a near-by bush. He stuck it on the end of an old blunt arrow. He wanted to be sure he didn't hurt Charlie. Jimmy moved forward slowly. He dodged quietly from tree to tree.

He peered around the trunk of a huge tree. There stood his twin brother. Charlie was slender like Jimmy, but he had a mop of brown hair, while Jimmy's was black as a pinching bug. Both boys were wearing only overall pants on this warm fall day.

Charlie, too, was out with his bow, in search of game, but he hadn't heard his twin approach.

Jimmy raised his bow. He fitted the arrow to the string, the arrow with the red haw on its point. He aimed and let fly. *Whisht!*

"*Atwi!*" shouted Charlie. He jumped in surprise. "Ouch!" The tiny red apple had whacked him squarely in the middle of his back. It stung a little, but had bounced off harmlessly.

With a yell Jimmy dropped his bow and charged in. He wrestled his brother to the ground and seized Charlie's hair in one hand. "I've got your scalp!" he shouted fiercely.

"Hey!" cried Charlie, grabbing Jimmy's arm.

"I'm a mighty Sac warrior, and I'll kill every Sioux in sight!"

Charlie jerked himself free. He scrambled to his feet. "We weren't playing war party!" he protested. "Besides, I was a Sioux last time. It's your turn to be scalped."

Jimmy jumped up from the ground. He picked up his arrow and threw away the haw. "You'll have to surprise me first. You didn't even hear me coming this time."

"I will, next time," Charlie promised. In a flash he darted off through the woods. "I'll beat you to the clearing," he called back.

Jimmy dashed after him. His bare feet flew

over the ground. In a moment or so he was running abreast of his brother. Both boys put on all the speed they could, but Jimmy charged ahead. He burst into the clearing first.

"Oh, you always win," Charlie said. He caught his breath. "Let's play leapfrog."

He bent over, his hands on his knees. Holding his bow and arrows in one hand, Jimmy vaulted lightly over Charlie's back then knelt down in turn. Charlie jumped over him and knelt again. Jimmy ran forward to jump. Just as he put his hands on Charlie's back, his brother dropped to the ground.

"Yi!" shouted Jimmy. He was about to fall flat on his face. His bow and arrows flew out of his hand. His legs kicked wildly in the air. Ducking his head quickly, he did a complete somersault and came up on his feet.

"Why, what are you doing down there, Charlie?" he asked. He did not even smile.

Charlie had tried to play a trick, but now the joke was on him!

Charlie grinned as he got up. "Aw, I can't catch you at anything today, but you just wait."

"I will," said Jimmy, chuckling. "And now I'll tell you about the possum I saw."

A CHIEF LIKE BLACK HAWK

The two boys walked toward the cabin on the far side of the clearing. Smoke rose from the chimney and mingled with the branches of tall oaks back of the house. Beyond these trees lay the farm. It was land given to the Thorpes by the government when the Sac and Fox tribe had moved to Oklahoma. Near by, a large river flowed lazily along toward the Arkansas border.

At the door of the cabin a slender, pretty Indian woman appeared. "Come on, boys," she called. "Suppertime!"

When the twins went in, their mother was stirring a large kettle over the open fire.

"Smells good," Jimmy said hungrily.

"Where's Pa?" asked Charlie.

"He's already eaten. He had to go back to the corrals. Some of his colts have broken out."

"I wish we could help him," Jimmy said. "He used to let George help before he went to school." George was the oldest Thorpe boy. He was now away at school on the Sac and Fox reservation.

"Your time will come in a few years," his mother answered. She filled one bowl. "Here, give this to Mary."

Jimmy took it to his three-year-old sister, who sat in the corner, patiently rocking a cradle.

"I'm sure Eddie's asleep now, Mary," said her mother. "You eat your supper." She handed the twins their bowls. Then she sat down and picked up the moccasin she was making. "How did the hunting go today?" she asked.

Jimmy swallowed hard. "All I could shoot was Charlie." He sighed. "The animals are too quick. All except the possum and he's too slow."

"Tell Ma about the possum," Charlie urged.

Jimmy told his story again. He told every detail, even about the last bit of possum he had seen—the funny bare tail dragging along.

His mother smiled. "Did I ever tell you how the opossum got his tail?"

"No!" Jimmy answered.

"Tell us, Ma!" Charlie begged.

"Well, this happened long, long ago, you understand. It was in the early days, when the animals ruled the world. That was before the Great Spirit brought the Red Man into the forests. In those days *Ai-yani*, the opossum, had a bushy, beautiful tail."

The children ate as quietly as possible. They didn't want to miss a word.

"Now this is how the story goes. Once an

opossum was walking along. He saw a skunk coming. The opossum sang a little song.

> " 'Oh, you skunk over there.
> If I tread on your toes,
> You'll smell so strong
> That it will hurt my nose!' "

The boys looked at each other and both laughed. Well they knew about the skunk! Many times they had startled one, only to be chased away by the strong odor it threw out.

Their mother went on. "When the skunk heard this song, he wept. It had hurt his feelings. The opossum said, 'Why don't you sing to me?'

"So the skunk sang this song:

> " 'O opossum, begone!
> But look back without fail;
> You'll soon see a snake
> Instead of a tail.'

"The opossum started to run. He ran away at

21

top speed. Then he glanced back. Lo! sure enough, his tail looked just like a snake! What had become of his beautiful bushy tail? The opossum ran faster. But whenever he looked back, there was the snake, always following him. He had worn his tail off smooth in the running, you see—the tail that was once as pretty as a fox's. Ever since then, *Ai-yani* has had the tail of a snake."

The children, even little Mary, were all laughing. "Oh, I'd like to see a possum run that fast!" Jimmy said. He thought of the way his fat, lazy *Ai-yani* had waddled along.

"That was a good story, Ma," said Charlie. "Tell another!"

Suddenly Jimmy said, "Even *Ai-yani* has an Indian name. Why don't I have one? Why is my name Jimmy Thorpe?"

"Well, your Grandfather Thorpe came from Ireland, an island across the sea," said his mother.

"My grandfather was a Frenchman, from a land across the sea."

Jimmy's eyes grew round and thoughtful. He wished he could go to those strange, faraway countries. He had never been farther than the woods near the Thorpe farm.

"Of course, all the rest of your ancestors came from our Sac and Fox tribe," Mrs. Thorpe went on. "So all you children have Indian names, too. Jimmy, have you forgotten that your Indian name is *Wa-tho-huck?*"

"Don't forget your great-great-grandfather, Chief Black Hawk," said a booming voice from the door. "His own people called him *Ma-ka-tai-me-she-kia-kiak.*"

"Pa!" shouted the twins. They ran to meet their father. Mary followed them to the door.

Hiram Thorpe was a huge man. He was tall and had broad shoulders. He was dark like Jimmy, and his black hair hung to his shoulders

23

in the Indian fashion. His boots and overalls were covered with dust from the corrals.

With his big hands he playfully rumpled each boy's hair. He patted Mary's head and went over to the cradle to look at the baby. Then he sat down, cross-legged, in front of the fire.

"Tell us about Black Hawk," begged Jimmy.

"My sons, you already know that he was our tribe's greatest chief, a famous warrior and a great hunter. Back in Illinois, many years ago, he led our people when their lands were in danger. He fought the Sioux and the palefaces and he won many times. When he lost, he lost with honor."

Mr. Thorpe stared into the fire. The boys sat quietly. Their mother had gone to put Mary to bed in the other room.

"Charlie, will you fetch my moccasins?"

Charlie went into the other room. Mr. Thorpe pulled off his boots.

"You youngsters are past five now. You're not babies any longer. You must think of Chief Black Hawk," he said. "You must try to follow in his path. Especially you, Jimmy."

"Me, Pa?"

"Yes, my son. All our people think you are like Black Hawk. You are slender and quick and handsome, just the way our oldest men remember the chief."

Jimmy stared at his father in surprise.

"It's not enough to look like a chief, my son. You will have to prove your own courage and skill."

"But, Pa, the Sac and Fox tribe doesn't fight white men or other Indians any more, and we live on a farm. How can I be a great chief?"

Mr. Thorpe gazed steadily into the fire. "It is true that times have changed. We live in the year 1893, as the white man counts the summers. But there is still much for a young brave to do."

Charlie brought in the moccasins. "What, Pa?" he asked.

"Why, both you boys must learn to hunt. You must learn to farm and to raise cattle and horses. You must go to school for the new learning that chiefs today need."

"But—I don't see——" Jimmy began.

"When he was a lad, Black Hawk was as active as the gazelle. He was as strong as the elk. He could track an animal for days and days without stopping."

Jimmy looked at big Hiram Thorpe. "Pa is like that, too," he thought proudly. "Will I ever be as big as Pa or Black Hawk?"

"The day you were born, the sun shone brightly on the path toward our cabin. So we named you *Wa-tho-huck*, which means Bright Path," said Mr. Thorpe. "Your time for great deeds will come. You must learn all your lessons well. You must be ready."

He stood up. "Enough of talking!" he said. "Now to bed. You boys have chores to do early in the morning."

Rolled in his bearskin in the next room, Jimmy lay awake a long time. He was thinking about Black Hawk. He wondered how he could ever be like that shining figure from the past. When he finally slept, he dreamed that the sun was casting its rays in a great Bright Path through the woods. With his bow and arrows he ran along the path. But where did it lead?

Fisherman and Hunter

FOR THE fourth time the Thorpe twins emptied their buckets into the water trough. "There! It's full," Jimmy said.

The pigs in the field were crunching greedily on the food he and Charlie had thrown out. There were acorns and hickory nuts and pecans the boys had gathered in the woods and corn from the barn.

"The chores are done. Let's ride before we go fishing!" Charlie cried.

Without another word, both boys raced for the barn. They stacked their buckets in one corner. Then out of the barn they went. In a second

28

they climbed up on the pasture fence. In the pasture two big work horses were cropping lazily at the grass. Jimmy gave a shrill whistle. One of the horses raised his head slowly.

Charlie whistled, too.

"Come on, Rip! Come on, Tear!"

Both horses ambled over to the fence. They stood a few paces away, pawing the ground.

"Oh," said Jimmy. "Maybe they're hungry!"

He pulled some broken ears of corn from his pocket. He handed one to his brother. "Come on, Rip." Jimmy held out the corn.

Now the horses trotted over and pushed to get at the corn.

"Yi, that tickles!" Charlie said, as Tear nuzzled his hand.

"Let's go!" Jimmy shouted. He grabbed Rip's neck and slid onto the horse's bare back. Charlie leaped on Tear. The boys nudged the horses with their heels, and away they went.

They trotted to the end of the pasture. In the
next field half a dozen wild horses were frisking
about in the warm sun.

"Look at that paint!" Jimmy sighed. "I'd
like to ride him!"

The spotted paint pony came to the fence.
He snorted at the work horses. Then he turned
and galloped away at breakneck speed. The
other broncos followed, bucking and rearing in
high spirits.

"He's terribly wild," said Charlie.

"I know, but Pa stuck on him yesterday. Pa
can ride them all!"

"There comes Pa now," said Charlie. They
could just see his big black hat as he rode along.

"Race you to the gate," Jimmy shouted. He
seized Rip's mane. He dug his bare heels into
the horse's sides. Bending low, he urged Rip
on. Across the field they loped.

Charlie gave Tear another hard nudge with

his heels. He slapped the horse's side with the flat of his hand. "Come on, Tear, we've got to catch Jimmy!" he begged.

Tear darted forward, and the two horses ran neck and neck. Each boy kicked and shouted to his horse, but neither could get ahead. Both Rip and Tear pulled up short at the gate.

Mr. Thorpe trotted up on his horse and dismounted. Before he said a word, he walked over to look at the pigs. He saw the corncobs on the ground. He saw the trough full of water. "You've done your work well, my sons," he said. "Now I must have those horses."

The boys slid to the ground. Mr. Thorpe took his horse to the barn and fetched harness for Rip and Tear. Soon the horses were hitched to the farm wagon.

"I'm going to bring some pumpkins from the cornfield," Mr. Thorpe said. "And where do my sons go this fine morning?"

"We're going fishing," said Charlie.

"Pa, could you show me—" Jimmy paused. "I—I can't seem to shoot my arrows straight where I want them to go."

"Fetch your bow in a hurry, then."

"I've got it right in the barn!" Jimmy rushed to fetch his bow and arrows. He and Charlie watched as Mr. Thorpe bent the bow to test it. It seemed like a toy in his long, strong hands. Quickly he fitted an arrow to the string. He pulled back slowly, aimed, and let fly.

Thud! The arrow had gone into a fence post.

"*Tshi!*" Jimmy exclaimed. "I think I know why my aim was bad! Shoot again, Pa."

Mr. Thorpe sent an arrow just below the first.

"Did you see, Charlie? Pa holds his left arm straight until the arrow is gone. I forgot that!"

"Why, yes," Charlie agreed, although he hadn't noticed.

Mr. Thorpe looked surprised. "You have a

quick eye, my son. Be sure to remember, next time. But don't go aiming at any bears!" He jumped in the wagon and drove the team away toward the cornfield.

"I'll remember," vowed Jimmy. He picked up his bow and arrows.

SPEARING BLUEGILLS

"I'll bet I can catch more fish than you can," Charlie said.

The twins walked past the barn and got their fishing spears. These were long sticks, forked and sharpened at the ends. Jimmy carried his bow and arrows, too.

"All right, but I'll bet I can beat you to the river!" cried Jimmy.

"No, let's go to the creek," Charlie suggested.

"With all those fish in the river so close by?" Jimmy argued with his twin.

34

"Oh, we fished there last time. Besides I know a good new place," said Charlie.

Jimmy shrugged his shoulders. "Let's go!"

They set off at a fast trot. They went through the woods, out across a stretch of open prairie, then into another patch of deep woods. It was more than a mile to the creek. Soon Charlie puffed and panted, but Jimmy jogged steadily on without ever slowing down. He loved to run even more than he loved to ride.

As the boys loped along through the prairie grass, the sun beat down in a warm and friendly way. The woods, when they reached them, were cool and inviting. They were full of signs and sounds of many different animals if you only knew where to look.

Jimmy caught sight of a sharp little face, masked by a black band. Then it was gone in the underbrush. It was *A-se-pan,* the raccoon. "I'll hunt raccoons one day," Jimmy thought.

The boys trotted up to the creek. They sat down on the bank while Charlie caught his breath. "See any fish?" he asked.

Jimmy smiled and nodded as a bluegill broke the surface of the water to snap at an insect.

"All right, you fish here, and I'll just go up around the bend," Charlie said. "When I come back, we'll see who has the most!"

"Charlie's up to something," thought Jimmy, "but I'll show him!" Aloud he said, "You'd better bring plenty."

As his brother trotted off, Jimmy picked up his spear. Quietly he edged closer to the stream. Soon his eyes grew used to looking down into the water. He sat motionless, watching. There were several little fish. Some darted and stopped, and some swam lazily about.

Then Jimmy saw a nice big bluegill. He raised his arm as slowly as he could. The fish darted away, darted back. "Now!" thought Jimmy.

Down came his arm, in a swift, sharp jab. Up came the spear again, and there was the fish, stuck on the sharp points. Jimmy put it on the grass away from the edge, so it wouldn't flop back into the water.

He looked and looked, but now all he could see were minnows. "Maybe I've frightened the fish away," he thought. Another good-sized fish swam in sight, but it was out of reach. Jimmy tried for still another, but missed. Time was passing, and he had only one fish! Then, all of a sudden, three big bluegills darted toward him. Jimmy speared one quickly.

He heard his brother coming.

"Didn't you have any luck?" Jimmy asked.

"Not much," Charlie said. "Only these."

Jimmy turned and stared in surprise. On Charlie's string were *five* bluegills. Each one was larger than either of his two.

"S-surely you are a great fisherman."

Charlie began to laugh. For a minute he laughed so hard he couldn't speak. Finally he said, "Yesterday I found a little pool where the fish are as thick as flies. I told you I'd beat you."

At first Jimmy was angry at being fooled. He didn't like to lose. Then he remembered what Pa said last night about Black Hawk. "When he lost, he lost with honor." Besides, Charlie was pretty smart to have found that pool! Jimmy grinned, "You certainly did beat me."

"I'll show you my pool," Charlie offered.

It was just around the bend of the creek. In a few minutes each boy had caught two more fish. Charlie looked up at the sun. It was near the center of the sky. "We'd better get home."

They set off for home, jogging through the woods and across the prairie. As they neared the woods again, Jimmy stopped.

"Here." He handed his spear and his string of fish to Charlie. He got his bow and a sharp arrow ready. "Watch for rabbits. I saw some here yesterday."

The boys walked forward slowly. Charlie almost stepped on an unseen rabbit before it broke away. It bounded high over a clump of grass. It stopped for an instant. Then it bounded off in another direction, stopped again, and poised to run.

Jimmy drew his bow, aiming carefully. "I must hold my aim until the arrow is well gone," he reminded himself.

Swish went the arrow. The rabbit fell over, caught squarely by the shot.

It was Charlie's turn to stare. "You—you got him! S-surely you are a mighty hunter."

"It's only a rabbit," Jimmy said modestly. But he was glad he had learned how to shoot straight.

Learning from Pa

ABOUT A year later, in the clearing around the Thorpe house, a large crowd had gathered. Many of the Thorpes' neighbors had come for a feast. The men had been away hunting for several days. Now the families of the hunters were sharing the celebration of a successful hunt.

Deer which they had brought back had been roasted over a big fire in the clearing. Everyone had eaten his fill of the venison, of corn and beans, corn bread and roasted pumpkin. Now everyone rested after the big meal. The women and children waited while the men discussed the contests they always held after such a feast.

40

"Good! It's about time for the games to start," Jimmy said to the other boys.

"We'll have running and jumping while there's still daylight." Mr. Thorpe marked a line on the ground. "We'll race from the pasture fence down to this line."

The other men nodded in agreement. They laid aside their coats and cartridge belts. Mr. Thorpe led the way toward the barn. He jogged along and motioned to the others to hurry.

"Why hurry now?" asked Mr. Gokey. He was a tall, broad-shouldered man but not nearly as big as Mr. Thorpe. "I'm going to save my strength for the race," he added.

The others shouted in agreement. Still, they trotted along to join Mr. Thorpe.

Young Louis Gokey nudged Charlie. "Just you watch my father. He'll win!"

"Oh, my pa can beat anyone!" Charlie answered. "Can't he, Jimmy?"

41

"Maybe so." Jimmy just knew Pa would win, but he didn't want to brag.

Charlie jumped up. The men were nearly half a mile away. "They're lined up, about to start!"

"Here they come!" Elmer Walker called out.

All the boys shouted as the men came nearer.

"See who's ahead!" Jimmy burst out. His heart was pounding as though he were running, too.

"It's Mr. Thorpe!" cried Louis. "Come on, Dad, catch him!"

Mr. Thorpe was out in front of the straining men, all racing at top speed. Jimmy noted how easily his father ran. Graceful as a deer he was, his long legs eating up ground at each stride.

Right behind Mr. Thorpe was Mr. Gokey. Jimmy noticed that Mr. Gokey seemed to be trying much harder than Pa. Mr. Gokey threw back his head and clenched his teeth, but he could not catch Hiram Thorpe. Nor could the others catch him. Slowly Mr. Thorpe moved farther ahead.

He sped across the finish line, his long black hair streaming in the wind.

"*Pa ki-meg ani-wi-san!*" Louis said with a sigh. "A mighty, swift runner he surely is!"

All the men shook hands with Mr. Thorpe.

"It was a wonderful race," said Jimmy, his eyes shining.

The boys talked away excitedly.

"I thought Mr. Gokey would catch your pa," said Clifford.

"Maybe he will, next time," Charlie said.

Rufus shook his head. "Mr. Thorpe is too big and strong. He runs like Black Hawk himself!"

Jimmy thought, "I must remember just how Pa runs. But will I ever grow as tall and strong as Pa or—or Black Hawk? All the other boys are bigger than I am."

It was true. Even little Peter, who was a year younger, was as tall as Jimmy.

"Shall we jump now?" asked Mr. Gokey.

"Someone is sure to beat Hiram this time," said Mr. Keokuk. "Maybe *Mo-ko-ho-ko.*"

All eyes turned to Mr. Duncan, whose Indian name was *Mo-ko-ho-ko.* He shrugged. "That is a great task," he said, "but we will all try."

Some of the men wanted to practice.

"Now who wastes his strength?" chided Mr. Thorpe. "I'm warmed up now. When the time comes, I will jump!"

The jumping line was marked off. Several of the men tried practice jumps. Then the contest began. Mr. Gokey went first. He ran for the jumping line as hard as he could go. Fists clenched, he leaped forward with all his strength.

The men all nodded approval. Mr. Keokuk marked the distance with a twig.

"A fine jump," Jimmy whispered to his twin.

"Not far enough to win," Charlie answered. "I am sure Pa can beat that mark."

Then came Elmer's father Mr. Walker and

44

Mr. Keokuk and Mr. Morton. None of them could surpass the first jump.

Now it was Mr. Duncan's turn. He took a long run. He made a mighty leap. His thin strong legs carried him a foot beyond the twig.

Mr. Keokuk rushed to mark the jump. "Now it is up to Hiram." He chuckled.

Mr. Thorpe trotted back from the line. He turned, stopping to measure the distance with his eye. Then he started forward. Faster and faster he ran. At the jumping line he leaped high in the air, so high he almost brushed an overhanging branch. The speed of his run carried him far, far forward. His heels hit the ground—a foot beyond Mr. Duncan's mark!

The boys all shouted at the tremendous jump. All but Jimmy. "Charlie! Did you see how Pa did it? He jumped higher than the others! See high—and far at the same time." Jimmy hopped about to show what he meant.

Mr. Keokuk shook his head. "I should have known—you can't beat Hiram Thorpe."

"It was Mr. Duncan's leap which made me go so far," Mr. Thorpe said seriously. "I didn't think I could do it—but I had to beat him."

"Who will wager on the wrestling?" Mr. Morton asked.

"Oh, ho! There are no such fools here!" Mr. Keokuk said, laughing. For none of the men could hope to throw Mr. Thorpe at wrestling.

It was nearly dark now. The fire mounted higher as the boys piled on fresh wood.

Mr. Thorpe wrestled each man in turn. Five times he faced a new opponent. Five times his strong arms reached out and placed an unbreakable hold on his man. Five times he pinned the other's shoulders to the ground.

Jimmy watched every action his father made. He was fascinated by the quickness and ease of his father's movements. "Can I remember all

I've seen tonight?" he wondered. Long after he was rolled up in his bearskin, he lived over again the excitement of the evening's sports.

FOLLOW-MY-LEADER

The next day was unusually warm and sunny. Most of the visitors had gone home the night before. Only the boys had stayed on to spend the day with the Thorpe twins. This was the last day before they had to go to school.

Now the riverbank echoed with yells and splashes. The youngsters dived and raced and swam about, as carefree as a school of minnows.

"Race you across and back!" shouted Jimmy to Elmer Walker.

Without a word Elmer dived in with him. They reached the other side at the same moment. But Jimmy turned more quickly. He pulled ahead as they started back. Just as he was about to touch the bank, someone grabbed him and pulled him under.

Elmer swiftly swam to the bank, climbed out, and stood laughing at Jimmy's bad luck.

Jimmy struggled and wrestled to get free of the clinging arms which pulled him down. He broke loose and thrashed to the surface for a deep breath of air. He could not see who had tackled him. He climbed up on the bank.

Charlie's head broke the surface. Charlie was

laughing so hard he swallowed a lot of water. He climbed to the bank and rolled on the ground to catch his breath.

"So it was you!" cried Jimmy. "And just when I was ahead!" He jumped at his twin, and they rolled over and over on the grass.

Charlie's shoulders were pinned to the ground. "I give up! I stopped you because it isn't polite to win all the time," he whispered.

"Oh, ho! You only wanted to duck me!" Jimmy answered. He laughed and rolled over to sun himself on the grass. The other boys climbed up on the bank to join the twins.

"You'd better have fun," said little Peter. "To-morrow you have to go to school—all but me!"

Jimmy jumped up. "Well, it's still today, so there's time for follow-my-leader!"

"I'll be the leader," cried Louis.

"Not you! We want a good game," shouted Rufus firmly.

"I'll show you a good game," Louis answered fiercely. He rushed toward the teasing boy, but Rufus dived quickly into the river.

"I choose Jimmy!" said Clifford.

"So do I!" said Elmer and Peter.

"Let's go, then!"

Jimmy grabbed his overalls and pulled them on. The others followed suit. Jimmy's mind raced ahead to all the stunts he could do.

He set off at a fast run toward the barn. Behind him, the boys trailed out, one by one. Jimmy raced into the barn. He scrambled up the ladder to the haymow. Up another ladder to a trap door in the roof! He pushed it open and crawled out.

Then he slid down the roof to the edge overhanging the pasture. Quickly he let himself down and hung from the edge of the roof. He dropped lightly to the ground. There was Tear, peacefully cropping grass.

50

Jimmy darted right under the horse, with a shout and a slap on Tear's flanks! By the time Charlie and Louis and Clifford and Elmer and Rufus had followed in the same way, the horse was bucking and rearing.

Little Peter was last, and he couldn't get Tear to stand long enough for him to run under. So Peter had to drop out of the game.

Jimmy clambered quickly up the pasture fence. He stood for a moment on the fence post. Then he jumped to the ground and ran on.

A sudden thought struck him. He turned a somersault, then doubled back toward the barn. He rushed up to an old, dry cistern. He flung back the rotting wooden cover.

The old brick walls were clammy, but there were plenty of loose places for hand and footholds. "Pa says to watch out and not fall in the cistern," thought Jimmy, "and I won't!" Carefully, he climbed down to the bottom.

He chuckled to himself as he heard the boys gathering up above. "Hurry! Here I come!" he shouted. His words echoed back and forth against the cistern walls. "Ho!" Jimmy thought. "Maybe I can scare them."

"*Ka-nag-wa, ka-nag-wa,*" he called in a funny high voice. "Bad luck, bad luck!" This time the echo sounded strange and ghostly.

"Listen to that! There are evil spirits in that cistern," said Louis. "I'd rather take a paddling than go down there!" He raced back to the clearing as fast as he could go.

Jimmy was laughing so hard he could hardly climb out.

Charlie, Rufus, Elmer, and Clifford snaked down the wall on one side as Jimmy climbed up the other. "Get ready to run!" he called.

He headed toward the clearing, loping along easily. In a few moments he looked back to see the four boys climb out of the cistern.

Now he ran faster into the woods. The cool shadows seemed to beckon him, but Jimmy was in a hurry. He wasn't moving quietly, looking for woodland creatures. *Sha-shag*, the garter snake, slithered out of his way. Birds flew up in alarm at the noise he made. *Ketshi-ka-na-na*, the chickadee, shrilled a warning.

At the edge of the woods Jimmy leaped into the lower branches of a huge beech tree. He climbed up to a long, strong limb. Out along it he went until it sagged under his weight. He dropped easily to the soft ground.

Without stopping, he was off again to the prairie. Just to run like this, fast and free, made his blood tingle.

"Now how is it that Pa runs?" he wondered. He thought of those long strides, the easy way his father dashed along. Almost without trying, Jimmy fell into the same long, easy stride. "I think I could run all day like this," he marveled.

He dashed into the next woods, up to the little creek where he and Charlie fished. Before diving in, he looked back to be sure the boys would follow him. It was a few minutes before Clifford came into view. Jimmy dived into the creek. A few strokes took him across. He ran upstream, dived in again and waited on the opposite bank.

He saw Clifford and Elmer and Charlie still following him, but Rufus was nowhere to be seen. Jimmy chuckled. "Rufus must have got tired," he thought.

He started off more slowly this time. He wanted to be sure the boys saw his next stunt. He went out into the prairie again, heading for a spot he remembered.

There it was, a long gully washed out by the spring rains. It was dry and deep now. Jimmy measured it with his eye as he ran toward it. It looked wider than he remembered, and his heart skipped a beat as he thought of jumping it. Still, after watching his father the night before, he wanted to try. "Here goes!" he muttered.

Jimmy speeded up. Running for all he was worth, he took off in a great jump from the near bank. Up and up he rose, as high and far as he could. For an instant, as he sailed through the air, he thought he would fall into the ditch. He stretched out his legs as far as he could.

Thud! He had landed solidly on the far bank. For just a moment he teetered on the edge. Then he caught his balance and staggered forward. He had made it! "Whew!" he gasped. "I would never have tried this last week."

He wiped the perspiration off his forehead as he waited to see what the other boys would do.

Clifford panted up, measured the distance, then stopped. Elmer and Charlie came right behind. They looked at the gully, then at Jimmy. Clifford went back to try, he ran to the edge of the gully—but stopped again. "T-too far!"

"What a jump!" said Elmer.

"I didn't know Jimmy could jump that far," said Charlie. He felt proud of his brother.

Jimmy raced for home. Sadly the other three boys circled the gully and trotted behind him back through the woods and into the clearing.

"You were gone a long time!" Peter said to them. "Did he stump all of you?"

"*Wa-tho-huck* had a Bright Path, all right," Clifford sighed, "but he made it rocky for us!"

"He jumped that big gully!" cried Elmer. "Weren't you afraid, Jimmy?"

Jimmy smiled. "Maybe, a little. But I had to try it."

He walked over to a pile of old boards by the cabin. He picked out a short, flat stick. "This will make a fine paddle. Are you ready to run the gantlet?"

Elmer was panting. "*Hey-yo!* Haven't we had enough?"

"Not yet. Let's go!" Jimmy was grinning from ear to ear.

He stood, spraddle-legged. He waved his paddle. One by one the boys dropped on all fours and crawled as fast as they could between Jimmy's legs.

Whack! went the paddle and "*Yi!*" went Charlie—and then Louis and Clifford and Peter and Elmer and Rufus. That was the way they ran the gantlet when they had been stumped.

"Who'll be leader now?" Jimmy asked. "I choose Clifford."

"Just you wait till I rest," shouted Clifford, rubbing the seat of his pants. "This time I'll stump you!"

School Days on the Reservation

"Now, Hiram, see that the boys don't get dirty before they reach the school," cautioned Mrs. Thorpe. She stood beside the wagon. Little Mary was clinging to her skirt.

"They shall not move from this seat until we get there, Charlotte," Mr. Thorpe promised.

The twins sat, straight as ramrods, beside their father. They looked at each other. Both boys felt ill at ease in their new clothes. They were wearing handsome buckskin suits that Mrs. Thorpe had just finished. The long pants were trimmed with fringe. The long, soft jackets had fringed edgings.

Jimmy touched the soft, light-colored leather of his pants. "My, our suits are pretty," he thought to himself, "but I can't wait to get my overalls on again!"

"I like the moccasins," Charlie whispered, "but I'd just as soon go barefoot."

Mrs. Thorpe was full of last-minute instructions. "Your overalls are in your bundles. Be sure to wear them for everyday. And remember, George will help you if you need anything."

"We'd better start, Charlotte," said Mr. Thorpe, "so I can be back for supper."

For several miles they drove through farm lanes until they reached the Shawneetown-Sac and Fox Road. Here they must turn and go north for twenty miles to reach the school.

They bumped along through woodlands, past farms, and over prairie. Charlie and Jimmy whispered together of the many sights along the way. The twins tried not to show their excitement.

"Now we're on the Sac and Fox Reservation," said Mr. Thorpe. "This is the land the government set aside for our people."

He said no more. He was not in a talking mood. He seldom was, until the day's chores were done and the firelight danced.

Now the excitement of the journey began to grow less for Jimmy. Miles rolled past under the horses' hoofs. Farther and farther they traveled, away from the farm and the cabin and the woods and streams he knew so well.

Lonesomeness crept over Jimmy. How could he have been so eager to travel to the far places of the earth? Then he remembered that this was the path he must take. Pa had said he must have the new learning, if he ever hoped to follow in the steps of Black Hawk. Jimmy set his jaw.

He stole a glance at Charlie. His brother was staring straight ahead. Jimmy could tell that Charlie was homesick, too. Jimmy didn't feel so lonely, then, for Charlie and he would always be together. Jimmy smiled to himself.

"Aw," he thought, "how could I be such a baby? I'm six and a half years old! All the other boys will be at school. George has been there for four years. I must stop being so foolish, or I'll never grow up to be a chief."

Just ahead now lay the buildings of the Sac and Fox school. Jimmy's eyes lighted up. Maybe this wouldn't be so bad, after all!

"My sons, here is where I shall leave you," said Mr. Thorpe.

They drew up in front of a two-story frame house. Other wagons and boys were there. Jimmy saw Louis Gokey—and he caught his breath. Louis was dressed up, too—but his buckskin suit was a rainbow of colors, covered with embroidery and shining beads.

Jimmy and Charlie jumped down, to meet a tall, slender, smiling young woman.

"Miss Patrick," said Mr. Thorpe, "these are my twins, Jimmy and Charlie."

"More Thorpes!" she said. "That is splendid, since we already like George so much."

She went on to greet the other new pupils.

"Good-by, boys," said Mr. Thorpe. "See that you learn much. Your mother and I wish to be proud of you. And you must be proud of yourselves." He patted each one on the shoulder, climbed in his wagon, and drove away.

Miss Patrick returned with Rufus and Clifford and Elmer and a number of other boys. "Bring your clothes upstairs," she said.

Miss Patrick led the boys to the second floor to a very large room called a dormitory. In it there were row on row of beds.

"Oh, Katie!" Miss Patrick called.

In came an Indian girl about nineteen years old. She had a nice smile.

"Katie, these are the new boys," said Miss

Patrick. "Katie will look after all of you in this dormitory," she explained to the boys.

Katie asked all their names. She assigned each boy a bed and helped put his clothes away. The youngsters inspected the room curiously.

Jimmy looked out the window. In the big yard beyond the schoolhouse a group of older boys were playing. They were throwing a ball and batting at it with a long stick.

"Look, Charlie! What are they doing?"

"There's George. Let's ask him."

Katie had heard the boys. "Why, they're playing baseball," she said. "Don't you want to go down and join them?"

Jimmy still felt strange in such a new place. He swallowed hard and plucked up his courage. "Miss Katie," he said shyly, "could we change our clothes now?"

"Why, yes, I think you should," she answered. "You go ahead, and I'll find you all again in time for dinner." Katie hurried out of the dormitory, so that the boys might put on their overalls.

A few minutes later the youngsters walked carefully down the unfamiliar stairs. Most of them had never gone up or down stairways.

"Whew! This is better," said Louis, touching his overalls.

"It certainly is," Jimmy agreed. "Let's go watch that game!"

They rushed over to the field. Eagerly the new boys watched their first game of baseball.

One of the older boys threw the ball. Another boy swung his stick, hit the ball and sent it high in the air. A third boy ran to catch it. "That's three outs," he called.

The players in the field all ran in. Two of them came over to the new boys. One was Ben Walker, Elmer's big brother. The other was George Thorpe. He was a tall dark lad who looked a lot like Jimmy.

"So you twins finally got to school! How do you like baseball?" George asked.

"It looks exciting," said Jimmy. "You never told us about it!"

"Well, it's hard to explain the game. You can watch now, but be sure you stay out of the way."

George and Ben went back to the game.

After a few minutes' watching, the younger boys still couldn't get the game straight. But they wanted to try it, anyway.

Clifford nudged Jimmy. "Go on, you ask George if we can play."

When the sides changed again, Jimmy raced up to George. "Will—will you let us play?"

Ten-year-old George drew himself up to his full height. "I should say not! Hasn't Pa taught you respect for your elders?" He looked so serious that Jimmy didn't realize he was teasing.

Jimmy tried not to show his disappointment. But before he could speak, George laughed.

"Here!" He picked up an old ball. "You can take this old pumpkin. Go clear down to the end of the field. And don't get in our way!"

Jimmy grinned. "We won't!" he promised. "And—and thanks!"

He looked at the ball curiously as he ran back to his friends. It was a squashy old yarn ball. The cover was cracked and frayed. But of course they could play with it!

"Catch!" Jimmy called. He sailed the ball right at his twin. Charlie grabbed it, and all the boys examined it. They watched the game until they understood some of the plays.

"Now, let's try it ourselves," Jimmy urged.

In a few minutes they had gathered rocks for bases. Clifford found a stout branch for a bat.

Rufus was puzzled. "What do we do now?"

Jimmy took a long look at the older boys.

"Let's see," he said, frowning. Then he told the boys where to stand. He put his brother behind their "home plate." "Now I'll throw the ball to Charlie, and you try to hit it with the stick."

Rufus took the stick and waved it fiercely.

Jimmy bounced the ball in his hands. Then he threw it toward the big rock that was home plate. Rufus uttered a loud cry and swung at the ball. He didn't come near it. The ball hit home plate and bounced—right into Charlie's hands.

Jimmy thought quickly. "S-strike one!" he shouted.

THE FLY HUNTER

"This—is—a—piece—of—chalk," said Miss Patrick.

Several weeks had passed since the twins' first day at school. About twenty boys of the primary class were sitting at their desks in the brick schoolhouse. It was a mild day, and flies buzzed in and out the open windows.

"Now, repeat it after me," said Miss Patrick.

"This—is—a—piece—of—chalk," the boys chorused.

Jimmy fidgeted in his seat. He and Charlie had learned English pretty well from their mother, but some of the other boys knew hardly a word. Long mornings of classes seemed even longer when the bright fall sunshine streamed through the windows.

Jimmy looked out at the distant woods. He wished he were stalking rabbits right now! He couldn't get used to sitting the mornings away. He hated to be cooped up inside.

"Now, Jimmy, you say it," Miss Patrick said.

Jimmy only half heard her.

"S-st! Jimmy!" whispered Charlie.

Jimmy was startled. Without thinking, he said, "This—is—a—piece—of—rabbit!"

There was dead silence for a moment. Then all the boys roared.

Miss Patrick rapped on her desk. "I know some of our boys speak English well already," she said, "but not when they don't pay attention."

Jimmy was embarrassed. He must be more careful to listen.

Miss Patrick announced the arithmetic lesson. She wrote numbers on the blackboard. She asked the boys to count. She gave them simple problems in addition.

"Oh!" thought Jimmy. "English is easy, but I can't follow these numbers!" Try as he would, he couldn't keep his mind on the lesson.

A fly buzzed lazily about and landed on Jimmy's desk. He tried to catch it with a quick grab. It flew up, then landed again. Jimmy reached in his pocket for an old strip of rubber he had found in the barn. Quietly he stretched the rubber, then let go of one end.

Zip! The end of the rubber snapped the fly, and it fell to the floor. "Oh, ho!" thought Jimmy.

"My aim was good. And I guess no one wants these old flies around."

Soon he was absorbed in flipping every fly that came his way. He didn't notice that Miss Patrick had stopped talking. He didn't realize that everyone in the room was looking at him, until he heard Rufus snicker again.

"Well, Jimmy, you have discovered something useful," said Miss Patrick. "Suppose you come back at playtime, after you finish your chores. Then you can get rid of all these pesky flies!"

Jimmy was thunderstruck—at playtime?—when he was planning to play baseball? Then he understood. This was Miss Patrick's way of keeping him after school. She was punishing him because he hadn't paid attention.

All through lunch Jimmy moped. The afternoon wasn't so bad, for all the boys had chores to do around the farm and workshops. Charlie and Jimmy and Elmer worked in the barn.

"Well, I have to go back and get rid of flies," Jimmy said at last.

"You can show Miss Patrick what a great hunter you are," Elmer teased.

"Besides, I'll miss the game," grumbled Jimmy.

"Don't worry, Jimmy, I'll pitch for you!"

Jimmy looked more unhappy than before. Charlie and Elmer went over to the ball field, while he slowly trudged back to the schoolhouse.

"Oh, Jimmy," said Miss Patrick, "the room is alive with flies! You start right in. I have some work to do here at my desk."

Unhappily, Jimmy pulled out his strip of rubber. He walked around the room, chasing flies. It didn't seem half so interesting now. "Well, if I must kill flies, I'll do the best I can," he thought fiercely. He squared his jaw.

Zip! Zip! Zip! He flipped the pesky insects steadily. For a few minutes he thought of nothing but his task.

"It's a home run!" someone shouted outside.
Jimmy edged over to the window to look out.

"Oh, Jimmy, there are so many flies right up
here behind the desk," Miss Patrick said.

Jimmy sighed. *Zip! Zip! Zip!*

"I guess that will be enough," Miss Patrick said

72

at last, in a friendly way. "You've done a good job. And I think you still have time for some baseball." She smiled at him.

Jimmy grinned sheepishly. "Thank you, Miss Patrick."

"And, Jimmy, before you go—I'm sorry I had to punish you today. But I want you to think about this. I've noticed how you take the lead on the playground. Why not set the boys a good example in the classroom, too?"

Running over to the field, Jimmy thought about Miss Patrick's words. "Truly it is a great task to be a leader like Black Hawk," he thought.

CHARLIE TO THE RESCUE

After the game, Jimmy kept wondering how he could do better in the classroom.

"Charlie," he said, "those numbers—they make my head dizzy. Speaking English is easy.

73

Chores and baseball are easy and fun. But not those numbers!"

"Does *Wa-tho-huck* like only the easy things?" asked Charlie. "I have seen *Wa-tho-huck* shoot a rabbit, make a long jump, and spear many fish. Can a few little numbers make him dizzy?"

Jimmy was startled. "Why, you—you talk like Pa, or—or Miss Patrick. What's the good of numbers?"

"When you take your furs to the Agency, how will you know if the trader counts them right, if you don't know your numbers? How will you know if you get enough money?"

Jimmy nodded. "That is certainly true." He thought for a moment. "Charlie, you talk just like a teacher. Maybe you'll be one someday."

"Maybe so," said Charlie. "I like school—just as much as baseball!"

"Why don't you teach me about the numbers, then?" Jimmy asked.

So Charlie told Jimmy all he had learned. He counted on his fingers. He drew the figures on the ground. He explained carefully.

"Now I begin to see!" Jimmy cried. His heart was full of gratitude to his twin. How could he pay back the favor?

"Charlie," he said, "would you like to be a better baseball player?"

"Sure!" said Charlie.

"I've watched the older boys who are good batters. I've learned a few tricks!" Jimmy grabbed up a stick lying on a rubbish pile. "Here! I'll show you all I know!"

A Shadow on the Bright Path

SEVERAL YEARS later the March wind swept through the clearing around the Thorpe cabin. It brought clouds of powdery snow. The twins were home from school for a few days. They were going on a hunting trip with Pa!

Early the first morning Jimmy and his father were out in the clearing. Charlie felt feverish and had stayed in the cabin. Jimmy was disappointed that Charlie had not been allowed to play outside with him.

Mr. Thorpe put some cartridges in the magazine of his big rifle. He handed the gun to Jimmy.

The rifle was nearly as big as Jimmy. But his

arms were strong, and he handled it as easily as he would his bow and arrows. He pumped the lever to move a bullet into firing position.

"You are nearly ten, my son," said Mr. Thorpe. "Do you remember what I have taught you about shooting? I want you to show me."

"Sure, Pa!" Jimmy felt excited. Many times Mr. Thorpe had shown the twins how to handle a rifle. Several times before, Jimmy had fired it in practice. Surely Pa would let him use it for hunting soon.

"Do you see the big knot on that dead tree?" asked Mr. Thorpe.

Jimmy nodded, hiding his excitement.

"Suppose that were the shoulder of a deer. What would you do?" continued Mr. Thorpe.

Without hesitation Jimmy raised the rifle to his shoulder. He sighted carefully along the barrel. He took in a little breath, held it. Slowly but firmly his finger sque-e-e-zed the trigger.

Pow! The rifle kicked up in Jimmy's hand, but the bullet had gone true to its mark. Jimmy wanted to shout, but he was silent as he lowered the gun.

His father's expression did not change. "I will waste no more ammunition on you," Mr. Thorpe said. "Remember, always try to know ahead what you are going to do in shooting or anything else. Then you are ready when the time comes." He started for the cabin.

"Will—will you let me shoot on this trip?" inquired Jimmy anxiously.

"We shall see," replied Mr. Thorpe.

Back in the cabin, Jimmy cleaned the gun very carefully.

Mrs. Thorpe was busy cooking dinner. Mr. Thorpe said to her in a low voice, "Jimmy is ready for deer hunting. When I show him anything, he remembers it perfectly. He is very good—for such a small boy."

78

Jimmy's heart leaped. He wasn't quite sure what his father had said. Maybe his father was going to let him shoot on this trip after all.

Mr. Thorpe checked over his gear for tomorrow's hunting trip—bullets, matches, food. Then he asked, "How is Charlie?"

"He is still lying down in the other room," Mrs. Thorpe said. "I don't know what's the matter with him. He still has a fever. I think the school doctor should see him. Mr. Walker is driving to the school tomorrow, and I'll send Charlie with him to the doctor."

Mr. Thorpe shook his head. "I can never understand why Charlie is not as strong as Jimmy. They are twins, and they have always done exactly the same things. Well, he couldn't stand the hunting trip if he is sick."

Jimmy felt very disappointed that Charlie would not be able to go hunting. He and his twin had never been separated before.

It was very early the next morning when Jimmy and his father saddled their horses. The buckskin suit in which Jimmy had traveled to school now served for warm hunting clothes. He had not grown much in the last four years. The clothes were still comfortable.

The air was still cold, but the wind had died down. Soon the sun peeped through the overcast and sent down a few warming rays.

"Bring me good luck this trip," said Jimmy, patting Rip's neck. "I'm just sure Pa will let me use the rifle!"

Rip followed behind Mr. Thorpe on Tear. They trotted away at a fast pace. Jimmy was thankful to be out in the open again. If only Charlie were with them!

On and on they rode. As they left the familiar countryside, Jimmy looked for signs of game. Once he saw three deer break cover on a distant

hillside. He called to his father, but Mr. Thorpe shook his head and went on. Another time Jimmy was sure he saw, through faraway bare trees, the awkward shape of a bear. But it was well past noon when Mr. Thorpe called a halt. "We will make camp here," he said.

They had stopped in a grove of trees, in a little hollow by a stream. Soon Mr. Thorpe and Jimmy were eating their lunch of bread and dried meat.

Finally Mr. Thorpe said, "There are many deer near here, many places where they come to get water. We will work upstream."

Mr. Thorpe checked his cartridge belt to see that it was full. He picked up his rifle. "Let's start," he called to Jimmy.

They walked briskly over a couple of small hills. Then Mr. Thorpe held up his hand. They were coming to a break in the trees. Ahead was prairie, dotted with clumps of trees along the winding stream. Without making a sound, the man and boy crept forward until they could look out over the countryside.

The wind had risen strongly now, in the late afternoon. It blew almost directly in their faces. "That's good," thought Jimmy. He knew that any deer up ahead would not be able to scent the human beings.

"*Pay-shakes-see*," whispered Mr. Thorpe, using the Sac and Fox word for "deer."

Jimmy saw it now. A stag was coming through the sparse trees by the water's edge. It was scarcely a hundred yards away.

Mr. Thorpe raised his rifle.

The big stag came into the open. It stood a moment, antlers upraised, as if looking for danger. Mr. Thorpe fired. The sharp report echoed and faded away. The stag fell.

They brought Tear down to the fallen deer. Jimmy held the rein. His father knelt and pulled the stag onto his shoulder. In one mighty heave he lifted it onto the horse. Jimmy whistled. He never ceased to marvel at his father's strength.

"Now we will have meat at the farm," said Mr. Thorpe. "Oh, a man must still be a good hunter! Then he doesn't have to eat his cattle and can sell them instead."

It was growing dark as they returned to their camp. Over a fire Jimmy and his father stewed some of their dried meat for supper.

Later, as the flames danced, Mr. Thorpe told of the old days when the Sac tribe lived up on the Mississippi River. In the whole Mississippi Valley no tribe could bring in more beaver skins, more otter and raccoon and muskrat and mink, more wildcat and bear and deer.

He told also of the days when he was a young man in Iowa. He told of the big summer buffalo hunts, when the tribesmen killed hundreds of the big animals for their hides and meat.

"But too many settlers came to Iowa," he

added. "That's why I moved here to the Oklahoma Indian territory."

Jimmy's eyes grew big as he listened. He was still eager to hear more when his father said it was time for sleep. Rolled in his bearskin, Jimmy lay awake for only a few minutes. He hoped that tomorrow he would get to shoot.

The next day, however, Mr. Thorpe did all the shooting again. He bagged two more deer and a small black bear. Jimmy jogged along all day, watching, hoping.

That night he looked at all the game. Surely they would hunt no more. There was too much meat now for the horses to carry. Surely tomorrow they would have to start for home.

But the next morning Mr. Thorpe filled his cartridge belt again. They started off. "I know of another place where many deer come," he said. "Keep a sharp lookout, Jimmy."

They went still farther upstream before Mr.

Thorpe paused. They moved slowly and quietly up a wooded slope. As they peered over the hill, Jimmy could see a bare spot by the stream. The hoofs of many deer had worn away the grass.

They waited. Ten minutes passed——a half hour.

Jimmy saw the deer first. He nudged his father as he caught a glimpse of movement far back in the woods. A big buck bounded along toward the water.

"Get ready, son," Mr. Thorpe whispered. He handed Jimmy the rifle.

Jimmy's heart gave a leap. At last! Now that the moment was here, he felt very jumpy inside. But his hands were steady. Up went the rifle.

"I mustn't miss now!" he thought.

The deer took a drink. It lifted its head to look downstream. In that instant Jimmy sighted. A steady squeeze on the trigger, and——

Pow! The explosion rang in Jimmy's ear. The

gun flew up in his hands, but the buck crumpled to the ground.

Mr. Thorpe looked from the deer to the small, eager boy beside him. "He will truly be a great hunter," he muttered to himself.

Aloud he said, "You have keen eyes, *Wa-tho-huck*. You will bring down many more deer."

"It—made a very fine target," Jimmy replied modestly.

"Well spoken," said Mr. Thorpe. It had really been a difficult target, but he didn't want to spoil his son.

He carried Jimmy's buck on his shoulder all the way back to camp and dropped it on the ground. They looked over all the game they had to take back home. Jimmy helped his father load two deer on Tear and the bear on Rip.

"What about the other two deer?" he asked.

"Give me a hand here," said Mr. Thorpe.

He knelt and shouldered one of the remaining

deer. Jimmy tugged hard, helped load his own buck on his father's other shoulder. Slowly Mr. Thorpe stood up. He staggered for a moment, then planted his feet firmly. He shifted the two deer into positions that would be more comfortable for him to carry.

Jimmy gasped aloud at the load on his father's shoulders. It seemed impossible. But Mr. Thorpe smiled. "Here we go!" he said.

He set off toward home. Jimmy led Tear. He gave a sharp whistle and Rip followed.

By sunset they had covered at least ten miles. Mr. Thorpe never looked to the right or left. He just walked steadily ahead. Jimmy had all he could do to manage the horses and keep up with his father. But in the crisp air he could have jogged along all day.

They made camp that night among scrub pine on a hill overlooking the stream. As their campfire leaped up toward the dark sky, Mr. Thorpe said gaily, "In the old days, when a young man shot his first deer, the entire village would gather for a feast. Perhaps we shall ask the neighbors to help eat your fine buck."

"I hope Charlie can be there," Jimmy said. He was eager to tell about the hunting trip.

CHARLIE WAS NOT THERE

The next day they started early. All through the cold, blustery daylight hours Mr. Thorpe pushed forward. He stopped only for lunch.

It was nearly dark when they reached the clearing and the little cabin among the tall trees. Mrs. Thorpe met them at the door. She wore her best black dress. Nervously she clutched her shawl about her shoulders.

"Charlotte! What's the matter?" asked Mr. Thorpe, as he saw her worried face.

"It's Charlie! Mr. Walker came back today

and told me that sixty children at school have measles. Charlie has pneumonia, too. It's bad. We must hurry!"

"I have to see Charlie!" Jimmy cried in alarm.

"What about Mary? And George?" asked Mr. Thorpe. They were both at the school now.

"Mr. Walker said Mary has the measles, too, but a light case. George is all right. Charlie is the one I'm worried about. Can we start?"

Mr. Thorpe and Jimmy hurried the horses to the barn and unloaded the game. They hitched two fresh horses to the wagon. In no time at all, Jimmy and his parents were driving toward the school as fast as the horses could go.

"How is Jimmy? Has he been all right?" his mother asked.

"There's nothing wrong with him," said Mr. Thorpe.

"Then he's lucky! He was exposed like all the rest, before he came home."

As the miles went by, Jimmy prayed silently for Charlie. Pneumonia—that sounded bad.

When they reached the school, they could see oil lamps flickering in many of the buildings. Hiram Thorpe drove straight to the house that was used as a hospital.

Miss Patrick met them just inside the door. She looked weary and sad.

"How's Charlie?" asked Mrs. Thorpe at once. "Is he all right?"

Miss Patrick shook her head. There were tears in her tired eyes. "Oh, Mrs. Thorpe, I'm terribly sorry! He was *so* sick. We—we couldn't save him."

"When—when did it happen?" Charlotte Thorpe managed to ask.

"Just now," Miss Patrick said quietly. "I had my arm around him and was bathing his face. The doctor was with me. We did all we could."

Jimmy could hardly understand what had happened. Charlie gone! He had never thought his twin might not get well. It was not time for Charlie to travel the long spirit road to his ancestors. Only when one was full of years did one think of such things.

How could there ever be a Bright Path ahead if—if Charlie was not there?

"You'd better take Jimmy back home," Miss Patrick said. "If he hasn't got the measles yet, I think he'll escape."

Football at Haskell

JIMMY looked out the window of the train as it neared Lawrence, Kansas. His face showed no interest. His first train ride had been exciting, at first. But it was not enough to keep him cheerful.

He had been lonely all that long spring and summer of 1898. Everything he did made him think of Charlie—swimming, fishing, hunting, riding, and even doing the chores. Most of all, just running through the woods, looking for stunts to do, he had felt deeply the loss of his twin brother.

Now Pa was sending him to school at Haskell Institute. Jimmy couldn't go back to the Sac and

Fox school. He just couldn't. "Can't I stay home and work on the farm?" he had asked.

"No, my son, a lad your age must be in school," his father had insisted.

"But not—not back to the Agency school!"

Mr. Thorpe had sighed, and then said in a kindly way, "Sometimes you are a stubborn boy. But there's a fine Indian school up at Lawrence, Kansas. I will arrange for you to go there."

Still, Jimmy didn't see how his path could be very bright, not without Charlie.

What had his father said?

"My son, when you follow a path, you must take one step at a time. One day you will reach your goal. And then it will be bright again."

"Maybe so," thought Jimmy doubtfully.

"*Law*-rence! *Law*-rence!" the conductor sang out loudly.

The train jerked to a stop. Jimmy started up in his seat. Time to get off!

A group of chattering Indian boys dashed for the door. They were about his own age, but somehow Jimmy hadn't been able to speak to them. He just didn't feel like talking.

Out on the station platform the boys, all in their best buckskin suits, looked around at the town. They didn't have a chance to see much. A stocky, smiling man with a weather-beaten face jumped down from a wagon near by.

"You boys for Haskell?" he asked. "Bring your bundles over here." Whistling merrily, he pushed the boys along. " 'Lias Doxtator, that's me," he said. "I'll see you boys safe to the school. Let's have your names now, boys. Lots of folks that don't belong to the school try to catch rides."

He insisted on boosting them up to the wagon.

"I'm Albert Thunder," said the first boy, as he tossed his bundle into the wagon. Then came Ignatius Iron Road, Joaquin Williams, John Snake, Jake Gohey, and John Splitlog.

Jimmy hung back until last. Then he scrambled into the wagon by himself. "Jimmy Thorpe," he mumbled.

"You're a spry one, for such a little fellow." 'Lias got up on the driver's seat and slapped the horses with his reins. During the whole two-mile ride 'Lias kept up his conversation.

Finally they turned in at the school grounds. Indian boys and girls of all ages were walking on the paths or running and shouting on the playgrounds. Haskell Institute looked like a town. It was bigger than Bellemont, or Stroud, or even Prague back in Oklahoma. Jimmy looked with surprise at the big stone buildings, stone houses, wooden houses, barns, sheds. "There must be more than thirty buildings!"

'Lias swung the wagon smartly around a circular drive and stopped before a fine big building. Down the steps came a short, quick-moving man. He had a bristling mustache.

"Well!" said 'Lias. "Here's Mr. Peairs, the superintendent himself, to meet you."

'Lias insisted on helping the boys down from the wagon. The superintendent greeted each newcomer. "Now, boys, you come into my office while I get your names," he said. "Then Pocahontas Howlett will take you to your quarters."

In a few minutes Miss Howlett, an Indian girl, took them up to the dormitory for young boys. She assigned their beds. "My, it's getting dark in here!" she said. She went toward the door and turned a switch on the wall.

Electric lights came on all down the length of the big room. Jimmy was startled. So were the other boys. They stood and stared. Not one had ever seen anything but kerosene lamps.

"How do you like our new electric lights?" asked Miss Howlett.

"Whew!" gasped John.

"They're magic!" said Iggy Iron Road.

"Maybe this is some of the new learning I must have," said Jimmy, half-aloud. "They're like thousands of fireflies caught in a jar."

"The new electric lights were put in only last year!" exclaimed Miss Howlett.

As the newcomers stood staring, another boy came into the room. He wore the school uniform: short pants and a jacket, trimmed with braid along the seams. He walked up to the bed next to Jimmy's.

"Jimmy Thorpe, this is Jonas Swamp," said Miss Howlett. "He'll sleep next to you."

"Hello," said Jonas in a very friendly way. "I just came here yesterday—from Wisconsin. Where are you from?"

Jimmy could hardly refuse to answer the smiling boy, although he still didn't feel much like talking. "Why, I come from Oklahoma Indian territory," he said. "My father has a farm there."

"Would you like to watch football practice?" Jonas asked. "My big brother plays on the team!"

Football? Team? Jimmy was interested. He did not want to tell Jonas that he had not seen a football game. "I certainly would," he replied.

"Come on!" Jonas urged. "Let's hurry! It's getting late."

100

They raced down the stairs.

"The field is over in back of the chapel," said Jonas. "Do you like sports?"

"Why—why, yes," Jimmy stammered. His head was swimming with all the new things.

He was even more excited as he watched the older boys playing football, while dusk crept over the school. Two lines of boys would charge at one another. Then they would run and tackle one another. Sometimes they would kick a strange-looking ball.

They were wearing odd padded clothes. Some of the boys even had padded helmets. Any sport interested Jimmy, and this looked like one of the best.

Finally the two teams lined up facing each other. One of the players shot the ball back between his legs. The player who caught it started off to one side. The boys on the other team piled in after him. Just when he was about to be

tackled, he slipped the ball to a tall, husky boy
who came tearing across the field in the opposite
direction.

The tall boy had a good running start. He
raced right around several players who reached
out for him. He set off down the field with an
easy long stride—just the way Hiram Thorpe
ran. Jimmy watched in fascination. The tall
Indian cut this way and that. He managed to
dodge away from every player who tried to tackle
him. He ran to the end of the field, and put the
ball down on the ground.

"A touchdown!" Jonas cried.

Jimmy was not sure what a touchdown was.
But he was thrilled by the way the tall boy had
run and dodged.

"Is—is that your brother?"

"Oh, no," said Jonas, "that's Chauncey Archiquette. He's new, and he plays end. He's mighty
good, too."

102

"He *looks* good," Jimmy answered.

It was getting so dark that the players started for the gymnasium to change their clothes. Jimmy watched Chauncey walking along.

"There's my brother James." Jonas pointed to a short, strong-looking lad who wore one of the funny helmets.

But Jimmy hardly heard Jonas. His eyes were on Chauncey. "I'll just watch him every day," thought Jimmy. "I'd like to play this game!"

JIMMY LEARNS BY WATCHING

Every day at practice time Jimmy hurried to the football field. Jonas and the others went to the small boys' playground. Now and then Jimmy pricked up his ears at their shouts. He was rather sorry to miss the leapfrog and follow-my-leader and races they were enjoying.

But football was something so new and so exciting he just *had* to watch. He had found out that Haskell had a school team. It played teams from other schools. Sometimes the team traveled to near-by towns to play, and crowds came to see the games.

Jimmy recognized all the plays by now and their positions. He studied the way each man played. James Swamp played guard, and so did big "Sal" Walker. Sal coached the team, too— and his skill in pushing aside the opposing linemen was amazing.

Then there was Walter Harris, the chunky Eskimo fullback. Short as he was, he charged like a wild bull. It usually took two or three tacklers to bring him down.

But most of all, Jimmy admired Chauncey Archiquette. He trailed up and down the side lines and studied Chauncey's every move. Jimmy would pat Varsity, the flop-eared dog that was the team's mascot.

"See! When he tackles, he hits hard!" Jimmy would tell the dog. Or, "There goes Chauncey on the end-around play!" Then he would just stand, openmouthed, and marvel at the easy way Chauncey's long legs covered the ground.

Soon the big end began to notice Jimmy. He would nod. One day he came to the side line.

"Hello, kid," he said. "What's your name?"

Jimmy mumbled his answer.

"Jimmy, is it? I guess you like football, eh?" Chauncey continued.

Jimmy was tongue-tied. But he nodded.

"Would you like to have a football and play a little yourself?" asked Chauncey.

"Would I!" replied Jimmy.

"Well, let's go see Mr. Robinson at the harness shop. That's where I work, and I'll bet he'll help us make one," suggested Chauncey.

Jimmy jogged along beside Chauncey. Mr. Robinson was about to leave the shop, but he was glad to give them some leather scraps and some old rags.

"Here you are, boys," he said. He hesitated a moment. "In fact, I'll just sew them together for you. You'd be here half the night, and I have to close up."

In his deft hands the old scraps began to look like a football. He stuffed in the rags, sewed up the ball, and tossed it to Chauncey.

"Thank you, Mr. Robinson. I'm going to train a new football star here."

"Have a good time!"

Chauncey flipped the ball to Jimmy. Without even thinking, Jimmy grabbed the ball and raced away. In high spirits, he twisted and turned, just the way he had seen Chauncey move. He turned and raced back.

The big end was surprised. He gave a low whistle. "Maybe I wasn't wrong about training a star," he thought. "The boy can really run!"

Now the small boys' playground was turned into a football field. There were enough boys for several teams, and Jimmy was having the time of his life. All day he looked forward to the athletic period.

But he was careful to pay close attention in class. Miss Mack was a very good teacher. He didn't want her to catch him napping. Jimmy often remembered what Charlie had said to him: "Does *Wa-tho-huck* like only the easy things?" He vowed he would learn all he could, though school wasn't always easy for him. Charlie had loved school so. "I must learn for him, too."

In the afternoons all the boys had chores to do. Jimmy and Iggy and Jonas had many horses and cattle and hogs to feed and tend. Working in the barn was really fun. Jimmy was always happier when he was active. It seemed like home to pull down hay and fill water troughs.

When 4:15 came, he was the first on the playing field. The football games were like pumpkin pie after a big meal, a real treat.

One cool October afternoon Jimmy and his friends were playing some of the older boys. Already they had two touchdowns, to none for Jimmy's team. Try as they would, the younger boys could not gain.

The two teams lined up for scrimmage. John called the signal for a kick. From his halfback position Jimmy looked across at the opposing team. There was Ernest Tredo, their best runner, playing back to catch the kick.

"I don't want Ernie to get the ball," thought Jimmy. "He's too dangerous. He might get loose for a long run."

John barked the signal for the play to start. Jonas, at center, sent the ball back to Jimmy. Jimmy grabbed the squashy ball, aimed for the side line, and kicked with all his might.

The ball didn't fly very high or very far, but it went over to the side where Jimmy had aimed away from Ernest.

Ernest had to run away over to get the ball. By the time he picked it up, Jonas and Iggy and John were upon him. With a burst of speed, Ernest dodged all of them.

Jimmy suddenly came running up and tackled him neatly around the knees. Ernest and Jimmy hit the ground with a crash. Jimmy jumped up instantly, but Ernest was slower. Jimmy grabbed Ernest by the arm and helped him up. Then Jimmy darted back to his position.

John was shaking with laughter.

"Come on, John, let's stop them now," Jimmy urged. "What's the joke?"

"It was funny to see you pick up Ernie," John answered. "He's about twice as big as you are!"

Jimmy hadn't thought about that. He grinned. "I thought maybe he was hurt."

Jonas laughed too. "You thought *he* was hurt? I was worried about you!"

The two teams lined up again. The older boys tried end runs, but first Albert and Jonas cut through and tackled the runner without gain.

Along the side lines Chauncey Archiquette and James Swamp strolled along to watch.

It was last down for Ernie's team. Ernie took the ball for a plunge right through center. Jonas was blocked. Ernie had a big opening.

"I've got to stop him!" Jimmy thought. Like a flash he dashed in from his halfback position.

Crash! He piled head-on into Ernie. They went down in a heap. Again Jimmy jumped up first, but this time he didn't try to help Ernie. His own head was swimming. Jimmy staggered around. He shook his head. In a minute he felt all right again. "Our ball!" he shouted.

On the side line, Chauncey gave a surprised whistle. "James, did you see that tackle?"

"I saw it, but it's hard to believe such a small boy could hit so hard."

The two teams lined up.

"It's almost time for supper," Jimmy thought. "We ought to make a touchdown quick."

He begged, "Let me run it, John."

"Perhaps we should let Iggy have the ball on the guard-back play," said John. "Perhaps——"

"Oh, go on, call something," Jonas said. "We can't wait all day."

John called Jimmy's signal. Jimmy grabbed the ball and started around end. "They won't stop me this time," he muttered.

Albert blocked out the opposing end. Jimmy swung wide. With a quick dodge, he got past the halfback. Only Ernest was in his way!

Running hard, Jimmy thought quickly, "Ernie is faster than me, but I can try to fool him."

Ernie charged for Jimmy with all his speed. Just as the older boy was about to crash into him,

Jimmy stopped short. Ernie's speed carried him right on by—he stumbled and fell! In a flash Jimmy was running full speed again, and no one else could catch him.

With a big grin he planted the ball over the goal line. All his teammates ran up to slap him on the back.

On the side line, it was James Swamp's turn to whistle. "He looks like another Archiquette! Two feet shorter and two hundred pounds lighter!" he said with a smile.

"The boy will be very good one day," said Chauncey, "if he ever grows."

From Marbles
to Hurdles

SPRING was marble season for the small boys of Haskell. They all made their own marbles. Below the rose hedge at the edge of the school grounds was a clay bank. That clay was just right for making marbles. The boys would shape it into little round balls and dry them in the sun.

Jimmy and Jonas and Albert and Iggy pushed through the hedge one afternoon to see if their marbles were hard enough to use. There was John, busily making a batch for himself.

"Hi, John," said Albert.

"Be sure you don't pick up any of our marbles," cried Jonas. "By mistake, that is!"

The boys all laughed. They ran to look at the marbles they had made the day before.

"Ugh!" said John, frowning. "Who wants yours? They're all lopsided, anyway."

Jonas and Albert and Iggy had made twenty or thirty marbles apiece. But Jimmy had made only three: a big one for a shooter, and two more.

John jumped up. "Say, Jimmy, why did you make only three?" he demanded.

"Why, three will be enough. When we start playing, I'll win some more!"

"Some people like to brag," said John. "They talk and they talk, but it means no more than the wind up the chimney."

Jimmy was surprised. He hadn't meant to brag. "Why, I only told the truth," he said.

He thought suddenly, "Maybe that sounds like bragging, too."

"I—I mean—I always do win some—" Jimmy stuttered. That sounded wrong, too!

"Some people like to show off their victories before others," John said stiffly.

Jimmy squared his jaw. He was usually easy-going. He didn't mind being teased, but John wasn't teasing. He was accusing Jimmy of acting puffed up. "And I'm not," thought Jimmy.

"Oh, don't listen to John," Jonas said. "It's only 'Heap Big Wind' who wastes his breath on a hot day."

All the boys laughed. John did like to talk.

But John didn't laugh. Jonas's remark only made him angrier. "Some people," he said, giving Jimmy a push, "don't know how to behave. Some people——"

He didn't get to finish. He and Jimmy were rolling over and over on the ground.

"Watch out for the marbles!" cried Iggy.

But the boys couldn't stop. They rolled on John's soft marbles and ruined them all.

Jimmy was strong, and he fought hard. But

116

John was bigger. He pinned Jimmy's shoulders to the ground.

"Enough," Jimmy panted.

The boys got to their feet. They shook hands.

"Well, it was a good fight, anyway," said Jimmy, though he didn't like being downed. "And I—I didn't mean to brag."

"Whew!" John gasped. "For such a small boy, you're a good fighter."

Albert laughed. "Hello, small boy!"

The others all laughed and teased Jimmy. He flushed in embarrassment, but he grinned.

John said, "I'm sorry I got so mad." He turned back to his work. "My marbles!" he shouted in dismay. They were all squashed flat.

Now the laugh was on John. But the boys set to work to help him make more. "He must have plenty for us to win," said Iggy.

"The rest of the marbles are ready," Jonas said. "Let's have a game!"

The boys gathered up their marbles and ran for the playground.

"John can make speeches to his marbles while they're drying," said Albert.

John stood, openmouthed. For once he could think of nothing to say as he stood forlornly by his soft marbles.

ALL SPORTS LOOK GOOD TO JIMMY

After supper the next evening everyone in school went out to enjoy the fine weather. The girls strolled back and forth between their dormitory and the office. On the chapel steps the band tootled away. It was learning new tunes for Commencement Day.

Over on one playground the baseball team was practicing. On the new athletic field many of the bigger boys were limbering up for the track and field contests to be held on Commencement Day.

Jimmy and his friends walked along, looking around. They couldn't decide what to do.

"How about a baseball game?" Jonas suggested. "Or maybe some more marbles? How about you, John? Want to play marbles?"

Albert chuckled. "John has lost his already!"

Jimmy couldn't help smiling. His pockets were full of marbles! He had beaten everybody.

"Do you need some marbles, John?" he asked innocently. "I think I have a few extra."

The boys all laughed and teased John.

"Here you are, John." Jimmy gave him several handfuls of marbles.

"Well," said John, "these will soon be back in your pockets, Jimmy. But it'll make a better game if I have some to begin with."

The boys stopped at the athletic field. "Let's watch for a minute," Jimmy said. "How many races do they have at Commencement?"

"Oh, they have everything!" Jonas answered.

120

"Hundred-yard dash, two-hundred-yard dash, potato race, and the hop, skip, and jump."

"And the broad jump and high jump and baseball throw and shot-put," Iggy added.

"We ought to try those things, too," said Jimmy. "That would be fun."

"I guess there isn't any sport you don't like," said Jonas. "Which race do you like best?"

"I like all of them," Jimmy said.

He watched the boys running and jumping. How he wished he were doing those stunts!

"And there'll be a hurdle race, too," Jonas remembered. "See? Ernie Tredo is trying it now."

Ernie dashed along the track. He vaulted the wooden hurdles, one after another.

Jimmy watched Tom Moonlight jumping and Walter Harris practicing hop, skip, and jump. Each event looked like more fun than the last.

"Why, those races are about like follow-my-leader," he thought.

He asked, "Would they let any of us try?"

"I guess we'd all have to grow some, first," Jonas said.

"Especially you, small boy." Iggy laughed.

"Then let's have some games of our own!" Jimmy shouted. "Come on, I'll race you to the playground!"

For several weeks, marbles and baseball were forgotten, while the boys ran and jumped and threw. As he tried all the different events, Jimmy kept thinking, "Truly, there is no end to the wonders of sport."

Jimmy is Inspired

In January of the following year, 1900, there was excitement at Haskell. The whole school was preparing to entertain important visitors. They were the famous football players from the Indian school of Carlisle, Pennsylvania.

In the small boys' dormitory Jimmy sat polishing his shoes. Jonas shined the brass buttons on his jacket.

Miss Howlett walked through the room to make sure each boy would be ready for the parade. "Don't rumple your uniforms," she cautioned. "There isn't time to send them back to the tailor shop for pressing."

Jimmy rubbed and rubbed on his shoes. He didn't want to look shabby in such an important parade!

"I think that's enough, Jimmy," said Miss Howlett smiling. "You'll wear those shoes out!"

Jimmy started on his buttons.

"I don't see why the team is coming all the way from Carlisle, Pennsylvania, just to visit here," said John. "It seems to me——"

"But they're not!" Jimmy said excitedly. "They're on the way home from California!"

"California?" said John.

"That's the truth!" said Jimmy. "Chauncey told me all about it. They beat the University of California on Christmas Day!"

"That's right," chimed in Jonas. "First they beat some of the big schools in the East. Then they were invited to California. And they beat them, too—the best in the West!"

"And some of the Carlisle players were chosen

for the All-America teams," added Jimmy. "They take only the best in the whole country."

"Surely they must all be great chiefs to do such things," John said wonderingly.

"Can you get to be a great chief by being a famous athlete?" Jimmy asked himself. He had always thought of sports as the greatest fun.

Perhaps sports were important, too, like schoolwork, and hunting, and farming. The Carlisle team had traveled all the way to California to play! All Haskell was turning out for a big parade in Carlisle's honor!

"Black Hawk was a great athlete," Jimmy remembered. "In the annual ball game of the Sac and Fox tribe he was always a leader, and his side always won."

"Hey! Jimmy!" Jonas called. "You'll never get finished if you sit there daydreaming."

Jimmy jumped. Hurriedly, he went back to shining his buttons.

The next morning school closed early. Promptly at 10:30 all the pupils assembled at the chapel steps.

Mr. Buch, the band leader, called the musicians to attention. The other pupils lined up in marching order. Mr. Buch waved his baton. The band struck up the Haskell song.

The musicians marched away. The pupils followed, joining in the song:

> "We will love our own dear colors,
> Their honor we'll uphold,
> While the Redskin stands defender
> Of the Purple and the Gold."

Around the circle they marched. On the steps of the office building stood the visitors. Mr. Peairs was there, too, with the welcoming committee from Haskell.

"Look how big they are!" whispered Iggy, nudging Jimmy.

"Eyes front!" Jimmy whispered sternly. But he, too, wanted to see the men on the steps.

The band changed to the Carlisle song. Then everyone marched into the auditorium.

A minute later the visitors and their hosts trooped onto the stage. Chauncey Archiquette was one of the welcoming committee. He had just been elected captain of the Haskell football team for the 1900 season.

Jimmy thought proudly, "I guess Chauncey is good enough to play with Carlisle if he wanted to. Haskell is lucky to have him!"

Mr. Peairs introduced the president of Carlisle, the famous Dr. Carlos Montezuma. As he looked at the tall, handsome Apache, Jimmy remembered what Pa had said. Times had changed for the Indian people, but there was still much for a brave to do. "I bet Charlie would have grown up to be a college president," Jimmy thought sadly.

Dr. Montezuma told of his experiences as an orphan boy, of his struggle to get an education. Then he introduced the coach of the Carlisle football team, "Pop" Warner.

Jimmy listened carefully. He did not want to miss a word spoken by this great coach.

"We've had a lot of good fortune in my very first season," said the stocky black-haired man. "We've won a lot of games. And it is a great pleasure to work with Indian boys."

All the pupils clapped their hands.

"My boys are not just football players," Mr. Warner went on. "Most of them excel in other sports. You don't find that in most colleges.

"Now I want you to meet our All-Americans. It is very unusual for All-Americans to be selected from any but the biggest universities in the East. So we are especially proud of Frank Hudson, our quarterback and great drop-kicker, chosen for the third All-America team!"

128

Frank stood up. Everyone clapped loudly.

"And Martin Wheelock, our tackle, on the second All-America team!"

Big Martin bobbed up and down quickly.

"And Isaac Seneca, our halfback, for the first All-America team!"

There was even louder applause for Isaac.

Mr. Warner then introduced all the other members of the team. "And let me say in closing," he added, "that we at Carlisle look on sports as one of the most important parts of our school program. First, we have our varsity teams. Then we have teams in all our different classes, for football and other games, too. Sports are an excellent way to bring out the good qualities in young men, and to develop good citizens."

Jimmy's eyes were wide. "There's nothing I love more than sports," he was thinking. "If only I grow bigger! I'd like to be a varsity player like Chauncey—or the Carlisle men."

That fall the Haskell football team was beating every school it played. It was Monday after their victory over the University of Missouri when Chauncey beckoned to Jimmy.

"Congratulations on the game," Jimmy said as he ran up. "I wish I could have seen it."

"Well, we'll still have several games on our own football field this fall," said Chauncey. "But I have some news for you. How would you like to play in a real game?"

"Me? You bet!" said Jimmy, grinning.

"The school has arranged a game for our younger boys against a team of Lawrence kids, this Friday," said Chauncey. "You're not as big as some boys, but I still want you to be a substitute on our team. How about it? Do you think that you would be willing to try it?"

"Oh yes!" Jimmy's heart was thumping with excitement. "Are you going to coach?"

"Yes," said Chauncey. "I'll come to your field after our practice is over this afternoon."

Jimmy was there early, eager for action. Chauncey had chosen almost all of Ernie Tredo's team to play for Haskell. Of the smaller boys only Jimmy was picked for the squad. He had to watch during most of the practice. Still, he was thankful just to be a member of the team.

"Maybe I'll get to play part of the time," he thought hopefully as he listened to Chauncey.

When Friday came, Jimmy was very proud to trot out on the fine new football field with the bigger Haskell boys. About half the school was on hand, sitting in the new bleachers. There was a cheering crowd from Lawrence, too.

All the players ran and charged up and down the field for a few minutes to warm up. Then Chauncey led Jimmy and the other substitutes to the bench. Jimmy tried not to show his excitement at being a part of a Haskell team.

The two teams lined up for the kickoff. On the field, the referee blew his whistle.

"Here we go!" shouted Jimmy. How he hated just to sit on the bench!

Ernie kicked the ball far down the field. The game was on!

The first quarter was very close and hard-fought. First Lawrence would gain, then lose, the ball. Then Ernie and his boys would gain and lose the ball. Neither side could score.

As the second quarter opened, Lawrence punted. The ball sailed high in the air but not very far. By the time Ernie had caught it, the Lawrence ends were right on him. They tackled him hard. Ernie went down. When he got up, he was limping badly.

The Haskell boys and girls groaned loudly.

"He's our best player," thought Jimmy. "I hope he isn't hurt!"

Chauncey went out on the field to talk to

Ernie. He bent down and felt Ernie's ankle. Then he motioned for Jimmy to come in.

Jimmy dashed onto the field. He looked calm, but he felt very excited. "Now's my chance!" he said to himself. "But with Ernie out of the game, we'll have a hard time."

Chauncey helped Ernie off the field. The two teams lined up.

On the first play Alex King, the Haskell quarterback, called Jimmy's signal. Jimmy grabbed the ball and started around end. His teammates Walter Bernstein and Joe Rapp were making interference for him.

Walter blocked the Lawrence end. Jimmy cut around to the outside, still following Joe. The Lawrence halfback and fullback dashed in. Joe blocked the halfback. With a quick twist of the body that he had seen Chauncey make many times, Jimmy dodged the fullback. Now only the Lawrence safety man was ahead of him!

All the spectators jumped to their feet.

"Come on, Jimmy!" shouted the Haskell boys.

"Stop him!" the Lawrence rooters cried.

Jimmy dashed down the side line at the top of his speed. The Lawrence quarterback angled over toward him equally fast.

In a flash Jimmy sized up the situation. "He has me cornered, but I know what to do."

He slowed down, just a little. The Lawrence boy slowed down, too. He reached out to tackle. Jimmy put on a burst of speed, dashed right past. He felt the tackler's hands grabbing for him, but he shook loose. Across the goal line he went!

The Haskell boys and girls whistled and cheered.

Alex missed the try for point after touchdown, but Haskell led, 5-0. The new rules of 1900 allowed five points for a touchdown that year.

All the rest of the half, Lawrence pounded at the Haskell line, trying to tie the score. When

Haskell got the ball, Alex called for more end runs by Jimmy, then Joe, then Walter. But the Lawrence team had spread out to stop the wide runs. Haskell couldn't gain.

On the last play of the half, Lawrence sent its star halfback around end. Running hard, he got past the line. He straight-armed Alex. Walter and Jimmy ran over to stop him.

Walter had a clear chance to tackle him, so Jimmy slowed down. All of a sudden the Lawrence boy dodged past Walter. Jimmy was caught flat-footed. The runner was crossing the goal when Jimmy finally tackled him. Lawrence had tied the score.

"What was the matter there, Jimmy?" asked Chauncey as the team rested between halves.

"I was sure Walter had him," Jimmy said sadly. "But nobody'll catch me slowing down again," he promised himself.

"Don't take anything for granted until that

136

whistle blows," Chauncey advised. "Now in the second half you'd better try smashes through the line. Lawrence is spread out to stop end runs."

"But it's so much easier to run around them," Alex argued.

"That's right," thought Jimmy. "It's no fun smashing the line."

"Well, Alex, you're the quarterback," said Chauncey. "I'll leave it up to you."

All through the third quarter the teams played evenly. Alex tried one smash into the line, but Lawrence stopped it with no gain. Alex went back to calling for end runs, and Lawrence stopped the Haskell runners every time.

On the last play of the quarter, Jimmy tried again to run around end. Two big Lawrence tacklers brought him down. He felt a sharp pain as his ankle twisted under him. As he got up he walked very carefully. "If Chauncey notices, he'll take me out," Jimmy thought in alarm.

He gritted his teeth and tried to act as if nothing had happened. He rubbed his ankle while the teams rested a few minutes between quarters. He felt more worried now about being stopped every time he tried to run the ends. He wanted so much to make up for his mistake! But he couldn't get free of the Lawrence tacklers.

"Alex," he said, "maybe Chauncey is right about the end runs. Don't you think we'd better try some more smashes?"

"We'd better do something," Walter said. "The score is still tied." The other boys agreed.

On the very next play Alex gave the ball to Jimmy for a smash through the line. Two big Lawrence linemen blocked his way.

"Well, here goes!" said Jimmy to himself.

He ducked his head and charged into them. They tackled him, but he was charging so hard they couldn't hold on. Jimmy stumbled through for a ten-yard gain.

138

"Why—why, that's just as much fun as running the ends!" he said. "I guess it pays to listen to the coach." His ankle pained him badly, but he was still eager to carry the ball.

Once again Alex called Jimmy's signal. He hugged the ball and charged forward. "Nobody tackles Jimmy!" he vowed to himself.

This time he bounced off the big Lawrence center, spun around, and headed downfield. He was knocked off balance, but he gained another ten yards before he stumbled and fell.

Then Walter and Joe carried the ball. Right down the field they went. Suddenly the Lawrence line closed up and stopped the Haskell charges at the goal.

"Let me take it!" Jimmy begged.

Alex called his signal. Jimmy charged for the line. Everyone was piled up in a heap. It was impossible to get through. He thought, "I guess there's no way but over."

Charging with all his strength, he dived over the mass of struggling players. Hands grabbed at him, but he went right on over. He landed with a thud—over the goal line for a touchdown!

Jimmy was so excited that he forgot to hide his sprained ankle. He hobbled around as the boys slapped him on the back.

As they lined up for the try for point after touchdown, Solomon LaPointe came dashing onto the field to take Jimmy's place.

"My ankle's all right," he protested to Chauncey when he got back to the bench.

"The way you charge into those big fellows, I don't want to take more chances. They could break you in two. You're a pretty small boy for the game."

"Huh!" said Jimmy glumly. "I wasn't being hurt! Please let me go back into the game!"

"Why didn't Alex call for those line plunges sooner?" Chauncey asked.

140

"Nobody wanted to smash," Jimmy admitted. "But you were right. Smashing is fun, too!"

"Well, there's always something to learn," said Chauncey, smiling. "Jimmy, your dive over the line showed quick thinking. It's dangerous—but it worked."

Jimmy felt better. He watched his teammates score another touchdown to win, 16-5.

Dark Clouds and a Big Chance

ONE AFTERNOON a few weeks later the younger boys were finishing their chores in the barn.

"Let's hurry over to the field," Jonas urged. "Not much of the football season is left."

"And we don't have much daylight, either," said Iggy. "Truly, the sun goes to bed earlier and earlier every day."

"Oh, Jimmy," someone called from the milking room. Mr. Hoyt, who ran the school farm, walked in. "Jimmy, you're wanted in Mr. Peairs' office right away."

"Y-yes, sir." Jimmy wondered why the superintendent wanted him. What could it be?

The other boys went out with him.

"What have you done wrong?" asked Jonas.

"Did you mash someone's marbles?" teased Iggy.

Jimmy still couldn't think of any reason. "I—I just don't know." He sprinted away from his two companions. He dashed up the steps of the office and knocked at Mr. Peairs' door.

"Come in," the superintendent called. He had a yellow paper in his hand. "Oh, Jimmy, I want to talk to you about something."

Just then Mr. Plank, who was in charge of discipline, poked his head around the door. "Could you step out here a minute, Mr. Peairs?"

"I'll be right back," the superintendent said.

Jimmy was surprised and worried when he saw Mr. Plank. "Oh, oh!" he thought. "I must have done something wrong!" He tried to guess what it could be.

He looked at the yellow paper Mr. Peairs had

143

put down on his desk. Could it tell anything? Jimmy's curiosity got the better of him. He picked up the paper. It was a telegram.

Please send Jimmy home. His father badly hurt. Hunting accident.

Charlotte Thorpe

Jimmy read it again before he could believe it. Not Pa! He was so big and strong!

Like a knife in his heart, Jimmy remembered Charlie. Then there was only one thought in Jimmy's mind: "I've got to get home!"

He dashed out the door. Down the steps, around the circle he ran. He didn't stop until he reached the railroad station in Lawrence.

A freight train to the Southwest was pulling out. Jimmy grabbed the iron rails on the side of one car, pulling himself up. A few minutes later the train jerked to a stop.

Jimmy jumped down and looked around. Up ahead the locomotive was taking on water from a tank beside the tracks. Jimmy didn't see any open doors on the freight cars, but at the end of one he saw a narrow ledge. He crawled up and stretched out. The train jerked again and started. Jimmy held on to the rough boards.

He couldn't sleep a wink all night. The noise of the wheels clacking over the iron rails was almost deafening. He had to hold on tight. Twice, when the train lurched, he almost lost his grip. Only his unusual strength kept him from falling. "I know now why it's dangerous to hop a freight train," he said to himself, "but I just have to get home."

As morning came, the train pulled into Wichita, Kansas. Jimmy would have to start walking now. The train went on west, but home was nearly due south. He knew because he'd heard Pa talk about Wichita. He set off.

Tired as he was, he jogged all day. He drank from streams along the way. He ate dry berries and bark. That night he lay down in a little hollow beside a river. He fell asleep instantly.

As it grew late on the fourth day of his journey, Jimmy knew he was near home. He recognized the woods where he had hunted. He urged his aching legs on, trotting faster as night fell. It was very late when he reached the familiar clearing. He dreaded what he might find.

Then he spied someone. Pacing in front of the cabin, clear in the moonlight, was a familiar figure. Jimmy's heart jumped. It was Pa!

Big Hiram Thorpe had one arm in a sling, and he looked thin and worried.

"Pa! You're all right!" Jimmy ran to throw his arms around his father.

"Jimmy! Where did you come from?" asked Mr. Thorpe.

"I ran home, as fast as I could," said Jimmy.

"You *ran* home?" exclaimed Mr. Thorpe.

"I—I rode a freight train part way," explained Jimmy.

"My son! That's dangerous. You shouldn't have done it—even though you were so worried." Mr. Thorpe scolded Jimmy.

Jimmy told his father about the journey. Mr. Thorpe looked at the small figure. He thought of the many miles from Haskell.

"But, Jimmy, the school would have paid your train fare home," suggested Mr. Thorpe.

"I—I never thought of that. I had to start at once. Were you hurt badly?" replied Jimmy.

"It is nothing." Mr. Thorpe glanced at the sling. "My arm was broken and torn a little." He paused and frowned. "But there is really bad news about your mother."

"Ma?" asked Jimmy.

"She has blood poisoning. I have taken her to the hospital. But the doctor says she—she cannot recover. There is no hope," answered Mr. Thorpe.

Jimmy was crushed. Just when he had found Pa all right—Ma sick—and not going to get well? He could not believe it.

"It is hard, my son, but we must be brave. Rest now. We'll go in the morning to see her."

Jimmy thought he would never close his eyes. His mind was in a whirl. But he was so tired he finally dropped off to sleep.

In his dreams he fought through a thick forest, trying to find a path. Great clouds hid the sun. He could see nothing bright ahead of him.

ONE STEP AT A TIME

In the weeks that followed, everything seemed wrong to Jimmy. Home was not home with his mother gone—first Charlie and now Ma. Even the river and the woods seemed unfriendly.

All the children had gone back to the Sac and Fox Agency school except George and Jimmy. George was sixteen now, and Pa wanted him to help on the farm. Jimmy worked hard at the chores. He hoped Pa would let him stay on, too. But one day in the barn Mr. Thorpe said, "It's time we talked about your schooling. Do you want to go back to Haskell?"

"No, sir." Jimmy could never forget that terrible day in Mr. Peairs' office.

"So be it," Mr. Thorpe said. "Tomorrow you must start to the new district school."

"But, Pa! You need me on the farm. Or I— I could get work on a ranch somewhere."

"Jimmy, a lad twelve years old should be in school. Your mother would want that. The new school is only three miles away. You can still help me here after school."

Jimmy didn't say anything. He stared at his father. He didn't really mind going to school, but he felt mixed up. Nothing seemed right. He felt so alone all the time. He did not really care what he was told to do.

Big Hiram Thorpe looked at his small son. He knew how Jimmy had suffered. He didn't want to be too hard on the boy. "It's about time you learned to ride the wild colts," he said in a kindly way.

"Pa," said Jimmy softly. "Do—do you think my path will ever be bright again?"

"Of course, my son! Remember, put one foot before the other, one step at a time. And your first step should be back toward school."

THE WOODS ARE FRIENDLY AGAIN

For the next three years Jimmy studied hard. "If Black Hawk could meet defeat with honor and lead our tribe through many misfortunes, surely I, too, can be brave."

He missed all the sports he had enjoyed at Haskell. Here everyone went home after classes.

Jimmy hunted and fished—sometimes with Pa, sometimes with George, but more often alone. He would jog along for hours, looking after his traps, and trailing game. Once again the woods seemed friendly. He learned more and more about the ways of animals. He brought home more game than George. He was almost as good a hunter as his father.

He learned to tame the wild colts that kicked up their heels in the corrals. He could do a man's work on the farm any day. He grew as strong as one of the wildest broncos off the range, but he didn't grow any larger.

Often he thought about Haskell and about Chauncey and the teams and their games.

"If I'm ever a great chief," he said to himself, "I guess it won't be in sports."

Many times he wondered about those words

he had heard long ago: "All our people think you are like Black Hawk. . . . We named you *Wa-tho-huck*, which means Bright Path." Every time he wondered, he knew he must still take one step at a time.

CHOSEN FOR CARLISLE

One day in May of 1904 Jimmy slid into his schoolroom seat as usual. Mr. Bills, the teacher, wasn't in the room.

When Mr. Bills arrived, there was a neatly dressed Army officer with him.

"Boys," said Mr. Bills, "this is Major Mercer of the Carlisle Institute. He's traveling through the Indian Territory to choose students for Carlisle. He's looked over your records and wants to talk with several boys from this class. George Butler, you go first."

George jumped up eagerly. He left the room

with the major. After George and the major left, the other boys sat tensely waiting and hoping to be called.

Carlisle! Jimmy could almost see before him Dr. Montezuma and Pop Warner and the All-American football players who had visited Haskell. What had Mr. Warner said? . . . "We have teams in all our different classes."

"Why—why, maybe I'll get a chance to go there!" Jimmy thought.

In a few minutes George returned. One after the other, three more boys were sent out. Jimmy's heart jumped each time a new name was called. There couldn't be many more.

Mr. Bills looked at a list. "Now, just one more. Jimmy Thorpe, will you go in now?"

Jimmy wanted to shout. But he did not change his expression as he walked out of the room.

"Jimmy Thorpe? You're the boy who was a

promising athlete at Haskell, aren't you?" asked Major Mercer.

Jimmy was startled. "Why—well, I played lots of games there."

The major studied Jimmy. He noticed that the boy was small, but he had never seen a boy with better proportions for an athlete. Jimmy had long arms and legs and strong shoulders. He

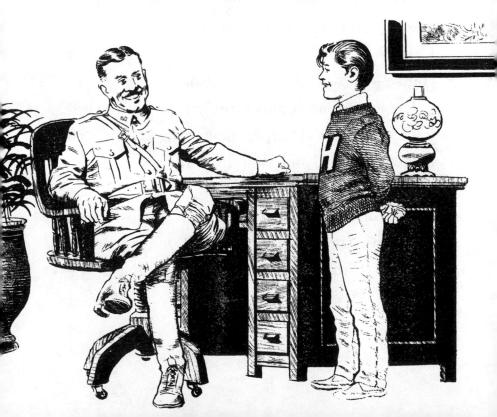

had better muscles than most Indians. They were not knotty or bunchy, but smooth and strong-looking.

"Sit down, Jimmy," said the officer. "You certainly have a good athletic build," he added. "It's not often I see a lad so evenly developed."

Again Jimmy looked so startled that the major laughed.

"You may wonder why I'm talking about sports. You see, we're proud of our teams at Carlisle. We like to get good students, of course—and good athletes, also."

He looked at Jimmy's records. "Let's see— 'James Francis Thorpe: height, four feet ten inches; weight, one hundred fifteen pounds.' It's too bad you're so small."

The major went on reading: " 'Age fifteen. Birthday, May 28, 1888.' Why, you'll soon be sixteen! H'm. Too bad. Well, we can't all be athletic stars."

156

"Maybe I'll still grow," Jimmy said.

"Well, that's not the most important thing, anyway. Let's see, now—you went to the Sac and Fox Agency school, then to Haskell, and then here." He scanned the papers. "You've done all right in your studies. Now, you've always done farm work at school. That right?"

"Yes, sir."

"Have you any idea what you'd like to study, if you came to Carlisle? We have many industrial departments."

Jimmy was caught by surprise. Then he suddenly remembered that day he had first seen the electric lights go on at Haskell. If those came from the new learning Pa talked about, maybe he could study that subject!

"Can—can I learn about electricity?"

It was Major Mercer's turn to be surprised. "Well, that's an unusual request, and very ambitious, but I'm afraid we don't have classes about that yet. You could be a printer, or a blacksmith, or a painter—or many other things."

"I—I don't know which——"

"Well, you can make your choice later. Jimmy, you have a good record. I think you're a promising boy. If you want to come, we'd like to have you at Carlisle."

"Yes, sir!" Jimmy was hardly able to hide his excitement, but of course no Indian could show his feelings before a stranger.

He walked out of the office with his head in the clouds. Pa had been right. If you took one step at a time, you found your path, and one day it grew bright again. Oh, how bright it seemed now! At a place like Carlisle, he'd have a chance to prove whether he could be a great chief, a man like Pa or like the great Black Hawk, even. *Wa-tho-huck* was eager to try.

Greatest Athlete
in the World

THE SUN shone bright and clear over the new Olympic stadium at Stockholm, Sweden. It was July, 1912, the first day for track and field sports at the fifth Olympic games.

Around the cinder track marched hundreds of men and women athletes. They came from twenty-six different countries from every part of the world. They strode along to the cheers of 30,000 people who had come to watch. The athletes went proudly past the royal box of King Gustav and Queen Victoria of Sweden.

Many other important people were in the box, too, to review the parade. Sitting together were

Colonel Victor Balck, president of the Swedish Olympic Commission, and James E. Sullivan of the American Commission.

The American athletes were just coming past the box. In the fourth row marched a tall powerful-looking Indian. He had a shock of black hair. His big square jaw was set firmly. His half-closed eyes stared straight ahead.

"That's Big Jim Thorpe," said Mr. Sullivan. "He comes from our Carlisle Indian school. He's one of the most versatile athletes we've ever had in the United States."

"Indeed!" said Colonel Balck. "I shall look forward to seeing him perform. We think that the champion athlete is one who can do many different things well. So we have the Pentathlon, five different contests, and the Decathlon, ten different contests, in all of which the same men will compete."

The colonel didn't have long to wait. The

very next day the Pentathlon was held. All over the stadium field men were warming up.

Big Jim Thorpe walked in with Pop Warner. He was one of the American team's trainers.

"Well, Jim, you're about ready," he said. "But I never expected you to be here when I first saw you at Carlisle. You were a skinny little fellow then!"

Jim smiled. He could hardly believe it himself. But in his years at Carlisle he had grown as fast as a milkweed in the spring, and as sturdy as one of the oak trees near the Thorpe cabin.

"Guess I'll jog around a bit to loosen up."

Mike Murphy, the head trainer of the Olympic team, came over to Pop Warner. "I'm eager to see how your big Indian does today. He can beat anybody in the United States, but these are the very best athletes in all the world.

"In every sport I've asked Jim to try he's always excelled," said Pop.

"You've done a fine job of coaching him," Mike said. "You're about the best there is at training athletes."

Pop laughed. "I didn't do much for Jim.

162

When I found him, all he needed was to grow. Look at him now!"

Mike nodded. "Over six feet tall and a hundred and eighty-five pounds of smooth muscle! You know, I've thought he was a little lazy on this trip. He's trotted around a bit. He's hardly practiced at all."

Pop Warner laughed. "Yes, but that's because Jim knows how to save his energy for the races. When he's in top condition, as now, all he needs is to loosen up his muscles. You'll see!"

The judges called for the running broad jump, the first event in the Pentathlon. One by one, the star athletes of the world took their jumps— Fred Bie of Norway, Frank Lukeman of Canada, Hugo Wieslander of Sweden, and many others. Finally it was Jim Thorpe's turn.

The big Indian walked slowly away from the take-off board. About twelve yards back, he stood quietly a moment to plan his jump. Then in a flash he was running at top speed. He jumped and soared high in the air. His great speed and the height of his jump carried him far, far out. Legs extended, he reached for every inch as he landed.

"Twenty-three feet, two and seven-tenths inches," one of the judges called.

People in the stands buzzed with excitement.

Each man got two more jumps, but no one could approach Jim's mark.

"The winner—James Thorpe of the United States," called the judge.

The American athletes set up a shout: "Rah! Rah! Rah! U. S. A.!" There was loud applause from the stands for Jim's fine performance.

He trotted over to the javelin field. There a group of Swedish spectators were cheering. "Here's where the Scandinavians will shine!"

When every man had thrown the long wooden spear three times, it was Bie of Norway and

Wieslander of Sweden who took the first two places. But Jim Thorpe was close behind them for third place!

Now it was the turn of the Norwegians to cheer. *"Hurra! Hurra!"* they shouted. "We'll beat the United States yet!"

But in the 200-meter dash it was Big Jim Thorpe who raced across the finish line in first place. In the discus throw it was Jim Thorpe who tossed the round flat weight the farthest.

"Rah! Rah! Rah!" U. S. A."

"Wait for the fifteen hundred meters!" shouted one of the Swedes in the stands.

Jim toed the mark for the start of this last race, almost a mile. *Crack!* went the starting gun. Two men dashed to the front. Around the first turn, they were twenty yards ahead.

"They can't keep that up," Jim said to himself. He held to a steady fast pace.

The second time around the track, the two

165

front runners were exhausted. Jim passed them easily. The third time around he was still ahead.

On the last lap he put on all the speed he had left. Fred Bie, the great athlete from Norway, struggled to catch him. For just a second Bie drew even, but he couldn't match strides with the big Indian. Jim drew ahead. He raced across the finish line, the winner!

"Oh, that Jim!" Pop Warner was smiling broadly. "Isn't he a horse, Mike?"

"Winner of the Pentathlon—James Thorpe of the United States," the judge called out. Up went the American flag on the winner's pole.

The crowds stood and cheered for Jim's great performance. The Americans shouted over and over, "Rah! Rah! Rah! U. S. A."

In the royal box Colonel Balck said, "Mr. Sullivan, I've never seen such a man. Four first places, and one third place, of the five events. Why, nobody will ever come close to that!"

As the days went by, American athletes won most of the prizes. All the other nations were certain that the United States would lose in the Decathlon. They still thought Europeans were best in all-round sports.

The Decathlon was held the last three days of the meet. On the first day Jim Thorpe won the shot-put. He made fast time in the 100-meter dash and a good mark in the broad jump. When the judges figured up the points at the end of the day, Jim was far ahead of the other twenty-two contestants.

On the second day he won the hurdle race. Then he won the high jump, and he ran well in the 400-meter race. Again he was far ahead in points at the end of the day.

"He *is* a horse!" said Mike Murphy. "You were right about him, Pop."

"This is nothing," said Pop. "Why, they ought to have some football, baseball, lacrosse, hockey, basketball, tennis, swimming, handball, skating, and target-shooting thrown in! Then Jim could really show you something. He's the best I've ever seen at all those sports, and more, too!"

On the last day Jim kept up his great records in the discus throw—in the pole vault—and in the javelin throw. Nobody could match his point total now! As in the Pentathlon, the last race was the 1500-meter run. Even Jim was a little tired by now, but off he started with his long easy stride.

"Why, it's only a mile to go," he thought. "I could run ten times that far." Once again he called on all his great strength and energy. Once again he raced across the finish line, the winner.

"Rah! Rah! Rah! U. S. A."

Panting from his hard race, Jim watched with pride as the United States flag went up on the winner's pole.

In the royal box Colonel Balck held out his

hand to Mr. Sullivan. "The greatest performance I have ever seen," he said. "Your Jim
Thorpe made eight thousand four hundred and
twelve points in the Decathlon, where even eight
thousand would be sensational. Again he won
four first places. Why, it is unbelievable!"

The winning athletes trooped up to the royal
box to receive their trophies. The King gave
each one a laurel wreath and a gold medal.

Jim Thorpe's turn came. The huge crowd
cheered itself hoarse, led by King Gustav himself. The tall, thin monarch shook Jim's hand.
"You, sir, are the greatest athlete in the world."

Jim gulped. "Th-thank you," he said.

The King handed Jim his wreath and two gold
medals. He gave Jim also a large bronze statue,
his own gift, and a silver Viking ship set with
jewels. It was a gift from the Czar of Russia.

Jim couldn't say another word. He just
nodded and smiled.

Never had he dreamed of such a day as this. Never had he imagined his path could be so bright. Perhaps he had proved himself worthy to be called *Chief Wa-tho-huck.*

CARLISLE DEFEATS THE ARMY

It was the afternoon of November 9, 1912. The stands around the football field at West Point, New York, were jammed. Only 3,000 people could get in, and many were turned away. The cadets of the United States Military Academy had a powerful football team this year. It was one of the strongest teams in the East. Army was favored to win this afternoon, too—over the Carlisle Braves, led by Captain Jim Thorpe.

But Carlisle had a fine record, also. They hadn't lost a game. They had beaten big colleges and smaller schools alike.

The cadets in the stands jumped up and cheered as the Army football players ran onto the field. There were several teams of them. All of the players on the Army teams were big husky boys. They spread out to practice kicking and running to loosen up their muscles.

"Look at that Devore!" shouted one cadet. "No wonder he's an All-American tackle. Two hundred and forty pounds—and all muscle."

Then the Carlisle players trotted out. There were just sixteen on their squad. With so few reserves, it looked as though they wouldn't have a chance against the many Army players.

"Is that the famous Carlisle team?" exclaimed a tall cadet corporal. "They don't look like much! They're so little."

"You're right," said another cadet. "I read that they average only a hundred and seventy pounds per man."

"That must be Jim Thorpe kicking!" cried

another. "They say nobody can stop him. He's a team all by himself."

"Well, he's not nearly as big as Devore. I'll bet our boys will chew him up today!"

On the field Pop Warner gave his last instructions to the Carlisle players. He slapped each man on the back. "Go get 'em!" he said.

The players trotted to their positions. Devore kicked off for Army. Thorpe ran over to snatch up the ball. Army players closed in on him, but he pounded ahead for fifteen yards before he was brought down.

"Stop that Thorpe!" chanted the Army cadets.

Jim grinned. He whispered to Gus Welch, the Carlisle quarterback. Welch barked the signals. The ball came back—to halfback Alex Arcasa!

Jim led the interference. He plowed into the giant Devore in a powerful block. Arcasa slipped through the line for a fifteen-yard gain.

"Wow!" gasped the tall cadet corporal. "That Thorpe certainly can block. But I thought he'd carry the ball."

Welch called out his signals. Back came the ball to Arcasa again. This time he slipped the ball to Jim on a crisscross play.

"Stop Thorpe!" shouted the Army players.

Two of them tackled him at the line of scrimmage. But he plunged right ahead, running for all he was worth, knees lifted high. He shook off tacklers and gained fifteen yards before two more Army men finally brought him down. Thorpe was almost impossible to stop.

Then Possum Powell took the ball for a gain. Next Arcasa was stopped. Jim took the ball on the crisscross again. He dodged and twisted for twenty yards before he was downed.

"Hold that line! Stop that Thorpe!" shouted the cadets.

On the next play the Army charged so hard

that a Carlisle player fumbled the ball. Quarterback Pritchard pounced on it for Army.

Right away, Army halfback Hobbs broke loose for a long run. The crowd was yelling, "Touchdown! Touchdown!"

But Jim Thorpe cut across from the other side of the field. Running like a deer, he caught the speeding Hobbs. He brought him down with a crashing tackle at the sixteen-yard line.

For a moment, Hobbs just lay on the ground, stunned by the tackle. Jim pulled him to his feet. "Nice run," he said.

Still Army could not be stopped. Yard by yard the West Point backs pushed the ball across the goal line. Army led 6-0, as Pritchard missed the point after touchdown.

Army kicked off to Carlisle. The Indians could not gain, so Jim Thorpe fell back to kick. He swung his leg into the ball with all his might. High and far it traveled.

There were "Ohs" from spectators at Jim's tremendous seventy-yard kick. Thorpe could do everything—better than anyone else!

After this the Army team could not gain. Hobbs punted, and it was Carlisle's ball on Army's forty-four-yard line.

"Come on, fellows, let's play some football now," Jim urged his team.

Arcasa slipped the ball to Thorpe on the criss-cross. Jim ripped off seventeen yards before the Army players pulled him down. Arcasa ran for a gain. Then it was Thorpe again for fifteen yards to Army's six-yard line.

"Stop Thorpe! Stop Thorpe!" yelled the cadets. Jim only grinned.

Welch snapped out his signals. The ball came back—to Arcasa. Jim led the interference, right through the Army line. He plowed across the goal with Arcasa right behind him. The score was tied, 6-6.

The two teams lined up for the try for point after touchdown. Jim stood ready to kick. Back came the ball to Alex Arcasa. Quickly he set it on the ground for the place kick. Jim's toe met the ball with a smack.

Up the ball went, end over end, right between the goal posts. It sailed off the field, he had kicked so hard. And Carlisle led, 7-6.

On the bench Pop Warner sighed in relief. "Whew! Well, I can always count on Jim when we need the points," he said to one of the substitutes. "I'll never forget those four field goals he kicked against Harvard last year. He kicked Harvard out of the national championship, that's what he did!"

Carlisle kicked off to Army to start the second half. Army could not gain. Keyes, the Army fullback, got off a high kick, straight into the arms of Jim Thorpe. The Army ends were ready to pounce on him. But Jim had started like a flash. He dodged so quickly that the Army ends missed him completely—and crashed into each other!

Straight down the field he ran, twisting and turning to avoid tacklers. Big Devore dived at him, but Jim pushed the tackle off with a mighty straight-arm. Two Army men grabbed him at the ten-yard line. But Jim was running so fast and hard they couldn't hang on. Every man on the Army team had tried to tackle him, but no one could stop him. He dashed across the goal line for a touchdown.

Even the Army cadets stood to cheer for Thorpe. One exclaimed, "Thorpe is everything they say—and then some!"

On the field the officials blew their whistles and waved their arms. "Carlisle offside! Score doesn't count!" they shouted.

A great moan came from the Carlisle stands.

Down on the field Jim said, "Too bad. That

was fun. Come on, Gus, let's get back those points!"

The Carlisle boys did get them back. They plunged and ran and pushed Army all over the field. Twice when the Braves couldn't gain, Jim Thorpe flipped a pass to Arcasa for a first down. Once Army tried a pass, but Jim intercepted. Everywhere it was Thorpe—running, tackling, blocking, kicking, passing.

He made two touchdowns and kicked the points after touchdown. Arcasa made another touchdown. Score: Carlisle 27, Army 6.

When the final gun sounded, the crowd jumped to its feet to cheer Thorpe and his teammates as they jogged off the field.

Several reporters rushed up to Jim. "Congratulations!" said one. "You'd be sure to make All-American again, if you'd played only this one game! Would you call this your best game of the year?"

"Oh, I don't know. I guess we all played pretty well today. But you'll have to ask Pop. My job is playing, not talking!"

Jim felt good about winning. But he wished everyone wouldn't make such a fuss about it! He walked on to the dressing room.

"You've got a great team, Pop!" called another reporter, turning to the coach. "What did you think of Thorpe today?"

"He played a fine game," Pop said. "So did ten other Carlisle boys."

"Is that all you've got to say—after that tremendous performance?"

"Just remember, if I do any bragging, you fellows will print it," said Pop. "You wouldn't want me to brag, would you?"

"Jim has a great scoring record," said another sportswriter, "but I never knew he was such a team player, too. Why, he's in every play, and he does more than his share of everything."

"Well," said Pop, "football players don't come any smarter than Jim. He doesn't try to hog all the glory. He knows football is a team game."

"You've coached him four years now. Is he the best player you've ever seen?"

"Well, I expect to see a lot more football players in my time!" answered Pop with a laugh.

"Quit kidding us, Pop. You act as modest as Thorpe does. I know he's the greatest player I ever saw—or ever will see!"

"Right! Right!" agreed the other reporters.

A CHIEF LOSES WITH HONOR

Back at Carlisle, about two months later, Pop sent for his football star one afternoon. The big Indian boy soon came to the coach's office. "You wanted to talk to me, Pop?" he ventured.

"Yes! Come on in," thundered Pop Warner. He was pacing the floor angrily.

"Why is Pop so upset?" Jim asked himself. "Did I do something wrong? Maybe it's all those reporters again." He said to Pop, "I—I hope there's not going to be any more fuss."

"You mean because you were chosen All-American halfback again, and scored twenty-five touchdowns and a hundred and ninety-eight points last fall? No. It's something else."

Jim guessed, "Some more famous doctors coming to take my measurements?"

"To find out what I already know—that you're a perfect physical specimen? No."

Jim couldn't understand what was wrong. "More baseball teams bothering you to sign me up?" he suggested.

Pop asked, "Jim, did you ever play baseball for money?"

Baseball for money? Jim stopped to think. "Why—why, yes, Pop. Two years ago, during the summer, down in North Carolina. It wasn't much. They gave us only fifteen a week, but it paid my expenses. I was really playing for the fun of it."

Pop Warner blazed back, "Only a professional takes money for playing. An amateur can't take a cent."

"Wh-what?" Jim stuttered.

"Why didn't you tell me? Don't you know the rule? Didn't you know that fifteen dollars a week made you a professional right then?"

Jim was startled. He had never thought of that. "Why, no, Pop, I didn't know. Other college boys were playing. Everybody knew it."

"But the others didn't use their own names!" Pop Warner exploded. Then he calmed down and smiled. "I've got to hand it to you, Jim, for using your own name honestly. But you should have known the rule."

"But does it make a difference? That was two years ago."

Pop sighed. "It means you shouldn't have been on the Olympic team. It means that the American Amateur Athletic Union says you must return your prizes and trophies."

Jim was taken aback. "But—but, Pop—— what does summer baseball have to do with competing on the Olympic team? Nobody ever paid me anything for running or jumping or throwing the discus and javelin."

"It's the rule. You aren't an amateur athlete if you've played any kind of professional sports."

Jim sat and thought. Try as he would, he couldn't see the sense of this. He had gone to North Carolina with a couple of Carlisle boys only for the thrill of playing baseball. He hadn't needed the money. He hadn't even wanted it. The other boys had needed it. Jim had had many big offers for large sums of money, but had never taken any of these.

"They—they want me to give back my

prizes?" It was a blow to his pride, after that great day in Stockholm. "All right, Pop," said Jim. "If that's the rule, they can have the prizes back. But I don't understand it. I never meant to do anything wrong."

He was thinking, "I've won lots of things and never bragged much about them. I guess I can lose with honor—like—like Black Hawk."

"I knew you'd see it that way," said Pop. "I'm mighty sorry for you, but we've got to stick to the rules."

"I—I hope they won't blame you for this," Jim said sadly.

Pop exploded again. "Why, you great big galoot, it's you I'm worried about!"

"What do you think I ought to do now?"

"Why—why—I guess you'll just have to accept an offer from one of the major-league baseball teams—the New York Giants, say. And there may soon be professional football. If you want to make your living from sports, there's no better athlete than you."

Jim thought that over for a minute. He still liked sports for the thrill and excitement of competition. But if he could make his living from them, too—— "Why, sure, Pop. That's what I'll do. If they say I'm a professional, why, I'll be one."

There was a knock at the door. A messenger brought in a telegram for Pop. He ripped it open and read it. He scowled. "H'mph!"

Then he grinned. "Well, Jim, this may make you feel better. They tried to offer your prizes to those Scandinavian fellows who won second—you know, Fred Bie and Hugo Wieslander. But they won't take 'em! They say they don't understand our rules, and you won fairly."

This did make Jim feel better. Bie and Wieslander were acting like great chiefs in refusing the awards.

186

"Even so, I—I guess I'll still have to give up the prizes?" Jim's heart would be heavy for a long time at this unexpected blow.

"Yes," said Pop. "I'll send 'em in to the Amateur Athletic Union. But you're still the greatest athlete. And you'll be a big success in any professional sport you try."

"Thanks, Pop," said Jim. He would be a success, he vowed. He must always prove himself worthy to be called a great chief.

Athlete of the Half Century

I⊤ WAS thirty-seven years later, one night in 1950. In a Philadelphia newspaper office, the sports editor was planning his next day's page.

A copy boy hurried into the room and put some papers on the editor's desk. "Right off the Associated Press wire," he said.

The editor glanced at the top sheet. "Well, a hometown celebrity! The coach of our Philadelphia Eagles, Jim Thorpe. Listen to this:

'Jim Thorpe, that almost legendary figure of the sports world, had additional laurels heaped upon his brow yesterday when the nation's sports experts named him the greatest male athlete of the half century.'

"Here's our headline for tomorrow," said the editor: "Jim Thorpe named greatest athlete of the last fifty years!"

"Say, that's fine!" said a chunky man at the next desk. "Everybody knows he's the greatest, but I'm glad they chose him while he's still alive to enjoy it."

HONORS FOR A GREAT CHIEF

Jim Thorpe was surprised when he learned of the new honors which had come to him.

He liked to think back on the fifteen years he had played professional football. Sportswriters said he had done more than anyone else to make it popular in America.

The big, slow-speaking Indian had helped start the first professional football league, back in Canton, Ohio, in 1920.

For six years he had played in major-league

baseball, mostly with the New York Giants. He had been a big league outfielder.

Now he was being honored for this wonderful record in sports, on top of his great college and Olympic career. First he had been chosen the greatest football player of the half century, and now—the greatest all-round athlete of the half century, 1900-1950.

The commonwealth of Pennsylvania selected him as the outstanding athlete in its history. The state of Oklahoma elected him to its Hall of Fame. Warner Brothers wanted to make a movie of his life. And the mayor of Philadelphia was giving a big dinner to present Jim with the keys to the city.

Little did he dream that soon there would be a city named for him too. Four years later the old towns of Mauch Chunk and East Mauch Chunk voted to become the city of Jim Thorpe, Pennsylvania, as a lasting tribute.

People crowded to congratulate him on his great record and honors.

Jim smiled good-naturedly as he shook hands. Memories of his old playing days had come rushing back to him. How bright had been his path in athletics! It felt good to be honored as a great chief once more. But how he wished he were young enough to play again!